E
UN]

Cheryl-Ann Hooper

The Five Year Lie

Dearest Phoebe,
With much love,
Cheryl xxx .

europe books

© 2021 **Europe Books**| London
www.europebooks.co.uk | info@europebooks.co.uk

ISBN 979-12-201-1545-2
First edition: November 2021
Distribution for the United Kingdom: **Vine House
Distribution ltd**

Printed for Italy by Rotomail Italia S.p.A. - Vignate (MI)
Stampato presso Rotomail Italia S.p.A. - Vignate (MI)

The Five Year Lie

Acknowledgements

Margaret Atwood once said about writing, 'If I waited for perfection, I would never write a word'. I think that just about sums up my approach to writing and completing this novel. Whilst I had the story for the book in my head, how it was to end or what was going to happen in the middle was a mere blank space which somehow evolved as the characters became real and their lives intertwined. Getting from words on a page to being published was a result of the numerous positive responses from friends and family who read the first draft and encouraged me. Thank you to Kieran and Chris, my writing group friends, who were the first to hear extracts from the manuscript and gave me the male perspective! Your comments and enthusiasm certainly contributed to helping me to write to the end and finish the story. Laura and Holly, my two daughters who read it and encouraged me to sign on the dotted line; Mary and Lucy for always being there quietly encouraging and supporting; Diane, Su, Sharon, and Tania for your positive comments, love and friendship. And finally, to Paul, my husband, for your support and for being by my side. However, none of this would happen without the insightful perspective and professional eye of the Europe Books team, in particular, Ginevra Picani, for commissioning the book and giving me confidence in my writing – your in-depth comments and feedback was invaluable. Elisa Giuliani for your support and guidance in the production process, and Luisa Maraffino for editing and proofreading – I cannot thank you enough for guiding me through the process and for your belief in me.

Cheryl Hooper

Twelve months, four friends, one decision

Sometimes the people who know you best, are those who let you down the most. Four friends, five years, one decision. A story about friendship, marriage, and secrets.

Introduction

December

   *"With a secret like that, at some point the secret itself
becomes irrelevant. The fact that you kept it does not."*
("Water for Elephants" – Sara Gruen)

Chapter 1

Carrie

Carrie opened the text, feeling the familiar thrill quickly followed by trepidation. Marcus's name came up as she surreptitiously looked at the message behind the computer screen in her office. Despite the large private office dominated by the dark oak desk, she knew this was wrong and something she needed to hide. She glanced down quickly.

"Hi, gorgeous! I can't believe that it's almost New Year's Eve! Do you realise it's 11 months, 29 days, and 3 hours since I last had the chance to show you what you've been missing all year?! What time can you get away?"

"Hello stranger, so you've finally remembered me then?" She texted back relaxing, knowing that this was going to be another session of flirting and banter between her and one of her closest friends.
"Ha ha! I work on the basis that absence makes the heart grow fonder. Missed me?"
"No, but I've missed your bad jokes."
"Lol!"
"BTW I've achieved my NY resolution of multi-tasking. I can waste time, be unproductive and, do nothing all at once."
"That's not funny!"
"Anyway, I've found a great place to go. How do you fancy champagne cocktails followed by oysters overlooking Chelsea Harbour?"

"I'd prefer Sydney Harbour but if that's the best you can do, I might be able to make it."

"Ha! Ha!"

The heavy oak door opened as the small round face of Carrie's PA appeared round the door. "Carrie, Linda Mwansa is here."

Carrie quickly glanced down at the phone texting "Gotta go!"

The phone bleeped immediately displaying another message. "Chelsea Harbour Hotel. Penthouse Suite. See you for breakfast on 31st. BTW, PJs not necessary!"

The shadow of the formidable civil rights activist walked across the room lit by the winter sun, towards Carrie with hand extended. They smiled at each other warmly and shook hands as Linda Mwansa sat down opposite the Human Rights Lawyer and looked at her directly.

"It's particularly good to meet you after all this time Carrie, I've followed your career closely over the years and know that my brother will be in good hands."

"I'm honoured to meet you Linda and hope that I can help, but you do know that I'm not as experienced as some Human Rights Lawyers out there. I'm sure there are plenty of better qualified legal representatives that would do an excellent job for you – Sir John Fisher is somebody that comes to mind, have you thought of contacting him?"

"Better qualified? I think not. Your qualifications easily match the highest legal names, Carrie. There might be Barristers who have more experience but what you have is passion and energy. I don't want somebody who is jaded or complacent". She paused choosing her words carefully, "I need somebody who really understands, and who genuinely wants justice."

Carrie sighed and sat back in the deep leather chair that almost engulfed her slight frame. Her mind racing, she quickly recalled the public case and media speculation over Thabo Mwansa, the young man accused of raping a South African woman whilst working as a junior doctor in a hospital. The dedicated Doctor had been accused of rape and put in prison awaiting trial, whilst the case had been presented as a done deal by the white South African woman who had started a social media campaign that had gone viral. She knew she was out of her depth but there was something about this case that wouldn't loosen its grip over her, and she had followed it with a hungry thirst for more information outside the public foray presented by the media.

A calculated risk taker, she considered the consequences of taking on the job pro bono and knew that from her point of view it was about setting a precedent for the future and defending somebody whose life would be shattered if found guilty.

"He didn't do it Carrie," Linda Mwansa said, shaking her head. "Believe me, I know my brother. He is not a rapist. He respects women. This is a clear case of injustice."

Carrie clicked the mouse to reveal the desktop calendar that had gone to sleep mode.
"The earliest I can make a start is in January. I have a few days holiday booked. Even lawyers need some

respite now and again!" She smiled, hoping that this high-profile client would understand.

"What's a few days here and there." Linda Mwansa replied, "He's been incarcerated for 6 months without a trial date. When could you start?"

"10th January?" Carrie said, playing for time.
"Thank you, Carrie, I'm very grateful." Linda Mwansa said, standing up.

"I will do my best Linda, but you know that nothing is guaranteed. I'll be in touch with the paperwork." Carrie said, shaking her client's hand.

"I know, I know. But at least I can sleep with the knowledge that he is in safe hands, my friend." Linda smiled warmly. She opened the door and looked back at her only chance of justice as she walked out of the room.
The heavy oak door closed softly, signalling to Carrie that she could check her phone again, heart pounding. One message: "Hi Cass. Looking forward to book club tonight and hope that we might talk through it from beginning to end for once! Vino contributions welcome! Rachel xx

She put her head in her hands and sighed. What on earth was she doing? An uncomfortable feeling swept over her as she tried to quell the guilt that was beginning to consume her.

Rachel

I am looking through my private scrapbook again, quietly turning the pages, remembering the journey Marcus and I have taken together. He doesn't know I have it. It's my secret. My memories. My babies. Temperature charts, calendars, car park tickets from hospital visits, pages from baby catalogues, colour swatches, scans, they are all here, carefully preserved. He doesn't know I named each one, even though they were the tiniest dot of a life unknown, and a soul that was yet to grow inside me. I read my diary entries noticing how they move from excitement and hope to despair and darkness. I never want to go there again, but now I find myself wondering, hoping, praying.

Life has just about returned to normal, whatever normal is, I think. I am sure that Marcus is secretly happy that it's over. There is no point going on and no money to continue. The emptiness and longing are beginning to subside, but I know that I will always feel incomplete. I close the book and hide it at the back of the bookshelf and stand up. The girls are coming over later and I need to get organised, need to sort myself out, need to put on my happy face.

Suddenly I feel nauseous as bile rushes from my stomach and reaches my throat. I reach the kitchen sink and throw up. I don't feel right and feel scared. My breasts feel sensitive, and I still feel sick. Can it possibly be? I am scared. I do not want disappointment and heartache again. I am scared.

I find the pregnancy test in the bathroom cupboard and check the date. Of course, it's in date! I buy them all the time. Three minutes, three hours, it feels the same but then I dare to look. It is positive. My disbelief manifests itself in tears. Filled with courage I try again – Positive! I am pregnant! Someone is looking after me, I know it. I hold the pregnancy test tightly in my hand and run downstairs.

***

Rachel pressed send to the group and smiled to herself looking around the pristine kitchen. Life was beginning to look good at long last. She patted her stomach and walked over to the mirror in the hall turning herself sideways as she smoothed down her T-shirt. No sign yet, not even the slightest curve of her belly she noticed disappointed. Never mind, plenty of time for that she thought trying to contain her excitement. After six years of failing IVF, she could not believe that she had found herself pregnant. Clearly, this baby was meant to be – just at the point of giving up all hope, her boobs had become sensitive, she felt nauseous, and there was a fluttering in her stomach. Was that excitement or the start of a new life? She squashed the possibility of misdiagnosis with an inherent feeling that she was right. She pulled the pregnancy kit out of its box and carefully read the instructions even though she had done this countless times before.

Marcus's car pulled up in the drive as music blared from the car stereo. He was in a good mood as he recalled the texts, he had exchanged with Carrie earlier, masking the stress and work challenges he kept hidden from everybody who knew him. He glanced up and saw Rachel at the kitchen window waving to him smiling. Seeing her face, his heart lurched as his emotions churned inside him. He loved her dearly but was it enough? Yes, he truly loved her but was he "in love" with her? In fact, what did that stupid saying actually mean? He slammed the car door and locked it using the remote without turning around.

Rachel opened the door beaming before he had a chance to put the key in the lock.

"Wow! Somebody's had a good day!" he smiled kissing her as he walked in.

She kissed him back passionately, eyes shining.

"Guess what?"

"What? We've won the lottery?" he said absentmindedly as he threw his jacket on the kitchen table and made himself a coffee.

"You could say that", she said, jumping up and down.

"Seriously? What do you mean?" Marcus said suddenly interested.

"Well, how do I say this?" she contemplated, trying to hide her excitement.

"Rachel just tell me what's going on!" he said, facing her as he put his hands on her shoulders.

"I'm pregnant!"

"You're joking? Are you sure? How can you be? The IVF stopped weeks ago."

"I know. It's just happened darling. It's a miracle! Can you believe it that after all this time, it's happened naturally!" Rachel exclaimed as tears formed making her eyes moist.

"Are you sure? Have you taken a test?"

"Ta da!!" she yelped producing the test result from behind her back, waving it at him.

"Darling, it must be a mistake. Perhaps you should check with the doctor before you go telling everybody, we need to be sure, don't you think?" Marcus said experiencing a roller coaster of emotions.

"Marcus, I am sure," Rachel said exasperated.

"My boobs hurt, I'm feeling nauseous and …well, I just know! I thought you'd be over the moon, but why am I getting the feeling that you're the one who isn't sure, not me! You do want this don't you?" she questioned.

"Of course, I want this!" he replied, walking over to her with his arms outstretched. "It's just that, well, I'd given up hope and now you're telling me that we are going to have a baby! I'm just getting my head around it." He said softly, speaking into the soft unruly curls that were the trademark of his wife ever since they first met, ten years before.

"I know! Can you believe it?!" Imagine, we'll be going to parent evenings at school, watching him or her getting a trophy for sport or performing in the school play along with the rest of them!" Rachel said, pulling away gaily pirouetting around the kitchen.

"Hey, steady on! I think there's a way to go first. Let's not get carried away," Marcus retorted, trying to contain Rachel's excitement as a slow thumping headache made its way to his temple. He opened a cupboard and took out two paracetamols and tried to change the subject.

"It's the girls' night in tonight, isn't it? I think I'll make myself scarce and go to the pub - that ok with you?" he said, swallowing the tablets.

"What? Oh yes fine. I've worked out that I'll be due sometime around September/October time! I've made an appointment at the doctor's tomorrow so should know for sure then."

"OK, good. Now if you don't mind, I'm going to change and go out for a drink with the boys. And Rachel, remember, don't say anything to anybody until we know for sure alright?" Marcus said, smiling to hide the strain on his face.

<u>Hattie</u>

Hattie glanced up at the clock on the kitchen wall and knew that once again she would be the last to arrive. It was the usual monthly book group cum girls' social at Rachel's house, the designated venue for their girly get-togethers because of its size and proximity to everybody's work.

She sighed and looked at the chaotic mess on the kitchen table. The twins had been gluing and sticking paper and plastic for a school project and the remaining debris reflected the over-zealous use of pink glitter that had somehow stuck to every crevice and grain in the worn pine table.

There is always payback for allowing and encouraging children to be creative she reflected cleaning up the mess. As a teacher and 'educator of young minds' as she liked to describe herself, it was her job to encourage and allow her two precious daughters to let their creative juices flow. But once again she was alone juggling between parenting perfection and trying to rediscover who she really was before the pressure of work, marriage, and children. Rob was away on police business that took him away for at least one week a month and whilst it gave them financial security, loneliness gave way to a longing to return to the days when they struggled for money but at least she had somebody to talk to about the minutia of her day, only in the way that partners do.

Hearing the doorbell ring, she raced to the door collecting a bottle of wine from the fridge and car keys on the way.

"I'm so sorry for the mess in the kitchen," she said apologetically to Hannah, the teenager from next door who had come to babysit.

"Oh, no worries! I'll sort the kitchen out for you," the young girl said, smiling as she walked into the Victorian hallway obstructed by a girl's bicycle, muddy shoes and an umbrella that lay haphazardly on the wooden floor.

"You are a Godsend!" Hattie exclaimed, pecking her on the cheek. "I should be back by midnight at the latest."

She ran to the small hatchback parked neatly outside the house and heaved a sigh of relief. These monthly meetings at Rachel's were like therapy and she desperately needed a dose of fun and frivolity. Why was it that despite having a close group of girlfriends who knew her inside out, did she feel the need for something more.

She turned the ignition on and looked in her rear-view mirror as her mobile-beeped a message. Two unread texts popped up on the screen - one from Rob and the other from Rachel. Shaking her head in disbelief she opened the text from Rob. 'Hi, sorry I'm not around tonight. I realised just now that it's your book group night. Hope Hannah is helping. See you on Saturday, love you R xxx.' Fighting back the tears that seemed to come so easily these days, Hattie shook her head in frustration determined to enjoy the evening and not dwell on the fact that her marriage was beginning to show cracks.

Jenna

Jenna's mum was on the phone again asking for help. It was the second call of the day and something that was beginning to become a common occurrence in the daily melee of Jenna's failing business, her money woes, and two children.

"Mum, I told you earlier today there's nothing wrong with your phone. I think the plug for the answerphone has been dislodged from the wall. There's no need for you to buy a new one. I'll come at the weekend and take a look."

"Did we speak earlier today, dear?" Jenna's mother said, trying to recall the conversation.

"Yes, mum, we did, but it really doesn't matter. Listen, I'm sorry but I have to go out in a minute. Can I give you a call tomorrow?"

"Yes, of course, dear, but don't forget my answerphone is broken and so you can't leave a message."

"Mum! I've just said it's not broken, it just needs to be plugged in," Jenna responded, trying to take the frustration out of her voice.

"Oh? Well, if it's not working by tomorrow, I'll get another one."

Jenna sighed heavily. "OK, mum whatever! I'll give you a call tomorrow." She put the phone down gently only to see her youngest son looking at her intently.

"Are you OK mum?"

"Yes, fine, darling. That was grannie. Everything is fine. Just go to bed and Jonathan will do lights off she said glancing across to her eldest son who raised his eyebrows as he put the kettle on.

"He's not a baby, you know! He can put himself to bed!"

She ignored him whilst searching for the car keys "So lights off at 10 then, OK?"

"Yes, whatever," Jonathan poured his coffee. "Just go mum and don't worry. It's Friday remember, no work tomorrow."

"Yes, I know!" Jenna smiled gratefully, wondering how she would manage without her eldest son who was rapidly turning into a man before her very eyes. Almost 18 he would be flying off to university in less than 6 months and then what? The burgeoning demands of her elderly mother were only just manageable because of his ability to keep her sane. She softly closed the door behind her hearing the sound of yelps and boisterous play fighting between the two boys.

***

Hattie leafed through the Little Coffee Shop of Kabul searching for the point of reference that was forming so much discussion later that evening. "I know it's here somewhere!" she exclaimed, peering closely at the open page whose words seemed to blur into a sequence of undefined shapes.

"For God's sake Hattie, put your glasses on!" Rachel laughed affectionately and grabbed the book off her. "Here it is!" She read the passage they were all looking for.

"Tomorrow is Thursday, and you will come to the bazaar. I am dreaming of seeing your eyes and praying to Allah that you will not be wearing your burqa. I know it is safer that way, but it makes me so angry. It's as if a woman's eyes, a woman's face, are evil. We who are old enough to have lived through one regime after another, know the burqa is about a man's fear, not about a woman's malice." ("The Little Coffee Shop of Kabul" – Deborah Rodriguez)

Jenna sat back on the worn pine kitchen chair and gulped the last drop of wine in her glass before pouring herself another, "I think wearing a burqa would make me feel anonymous in a good way." She said, reflecting on the passage. "Imagine walking around London without wearing make-up, doing your hair, and just going about your business."

"Jenna, if you hadn't just downed 3 glasses of wine, I'd be worried about you, my girl! Women have died to allow us to wear what we like, say what we like, and do what we like! Oppressive states like Afghanistan only get away with it because it is cocooned from the real world.

I feel sorry for the woman, and so should you!" Carrie said, trying to conceal the fact that she was furious behind the smile she had forced, to take the sting out of her words.

"Well, who rattled your cage?" Hattie laughed. "Someone had a bad day. We all know that Jenna's just winding everybody up for effect as usual."

Jenna shrugged and winked across the table mischievously knowing that Carrie would take the bait. "Anyway, they had been hiding their secret liaison for months from her son, hadn't they? Did you think they'd ever get it together? I didn't, and I was surprised when they made it public in the end. If I were her son, I would have felt betrayed and hurt that she didn't trust him enough to tell him."

"Ditto!" Rachel said, looking around as the others nodded in agreement.

"I need to get going," Carrie announced suddenly drawing back her chair. "Got an early start tomorrow."

"Hey so early? Come on Carrie, how about a coffee before you set off?" Rachel asked, concern forming across her brow. She got up to put the kettle on ignoring Carrie's wish to leave.

Carrie sat down again and looked at the others as an uncomfortable air filled the room.

"You OK Cass?" Hattie asked as Carrie smiled awkwardly, lips pursed.

"Yeh, sure. I am fine. I've just got a lot going on at work that's all."

Marcus

Marcus threw the leather holdall into the back of the Mercedes sports and slammed the boot shut. The crisp air showed his breath as the sun peeped its way through the clouds that lay low on the horizon forming a light mist. Water droplets clung to blades of grass and leaves, glass beads in the stillness of the winter morning, and what was the last day of the year. A whole year over, and what had he done? Wasn't that the lyrics to a song he wondered absentmindedly, admiring nature's beauty that was still possible in a London garden?

The bedroom curtains were closed as Rachel lay peacefully asleep, oblivious to the day ahead. It was New Year's Eve, and as usual, Marcus would be out until the last minute when of course he would turn up at the annual gathering of the gang, which this year was to be beyond the inner circle, and at a house party with additional friends.

She roused as the sound of the car engine revved on the drive as it pulled quietly away. Unlike previous years, his mind was drifting between the anticipation of seeing Carrie and the recent curved ball that Rachel had thrown by way of finding herself pregnant. It was five years since they started the illicit liaison that took place just once a year on New Year's Eve. Just one day, that is all he convinced himself, what was the harm in that? It is not as if they sleep together outside this. He had to admit to himself however, this was probably the most important and thrilling day of the year and one that he could not give up despite the nagging guilt that surfaced each December.

When did he see Carrie last? He recalled. The traffic lights turned to red as he slowed down on the approach thinking about her. Funny thing friendships with women he contemplated. A mate of his always insisted that men could never be friends with a woman without fancying her in some way. Was that true? He thought about Rachel's other girlfriends and whilst he could see the attraction in some of them, they did not have the spark that somehow Carrie ignited in him, such that they could playfully banter and talk for hours about nothing. These days it was rare to see her without the others, but before and during evenings out together, and at dinner parties, they always ended up laughing at one end of the table.

Marvin Gaye's 'Let's Get it on' played on the stereo as he found himself beginning to feel aroused. He pushed Rachel to the back of his mind and headed across Chelsea Bridge towards the hotel that he had booked. Facing the river, the prestigious building reflected the morning sun in its glass-fronted lobby dominated by a twelve-foot Christmas tree, decorated with hundreds of white fairy lights.

"I have an apartment booked." He said to the receptionist, who smiled warmly at him as he entered the building.

"Mr Welbeck?" I think your friend is already here. It's apartment 130 on the top floor."

He smiled to himself, remembering Carrie's need to always be early.

"Thanks, I'll make my way there myself. No need for a porter."

The door of the apartment opened just as he put the electronic key into its holder.

"You're late!"

"You're early!"

Carrie opened the door smiling. Her long chestnut hair lay loose to her shoulders that were covered by a thin silk shirt open to her navel that just revealed the slight curve of her breast. She was bare legged to the top of her thigh revealing pink silk panties. She stepped to one side as Marcus entered the spacious apartment taking her in.

"What?"

"You look amazing."

"Really?"

Her nakedness protruded through the see-through shirt as Carrie walked towards him smiling. "So, I suppose I should give you your Christmas present now, shouldn't I? Sorry it's a bit late." She said, biting her lip.

Marcus picked her up and looked around. "Where's the bedroom?"

"Next door"

He placed her carefully on the bed looking at her with shining eyes. "I've missed you Carrie," he said, unbuttoning her shirt.

"I've missed you too," she said, moving his face to her breast.

Chapter 2

Carrie pulled into the sweeping drive hearing the crunch of the gravel beneath the tyres. Snow had started falling and the windows of the detached cottage in the Chilton hills were festooned with fairy lights. The grand Christmas tree to the side of the oak panelled front door twinkled invitingly as revellers laughed and chatted in preparation for the midnight countdown. She began to question the decision to go to this party, which was seemingly in the middle of nowhere, as far as she was concerned. The hosts were former neighbours of Rachel and Marcus having turned evangelistic about their move into the country after living in London for ten years. What do people do for entertainment in these places, she mumbled under her breath, slightly uptight after the long drive.

Nine thirty-five and an hour later than everybody else, she was not in the mood to go through the façade of being with her closest friends yet again on New Year's Eve.

Seeing a space between two parked cars she pulled forward and reversed in absentmindedly catching the wing mirror of the black mini cooper to the left.

"Shit!" she moved forward in a panic and tried again. The prolonged grating noise against the parked car left a long scratch against the immaculate BMW and a slight dent on the black door of the neighbouring brand new mini. Carrie squeezed out of the driver's seat to look more closely at the damage and noticed the broken light. "Shit! Shit! Shit!" she muttered under her breath.

"A bit of T-cut should get that out" A calm voice came from the dark referring to the scratch on her car.

"I'm not bothered about my car, it's the other one I'm more concerned with. Do you know whose it is?" She looked up to see a tall shadow approaching and a pair of intense green smiling eyes watching her closely.

"It's not funny you know!" She said, opening the door, infuriated, and still trying to keep a lid on the guilt she was feeling from the earlier part of the day. "It'll be fine," he said taking a handkerchief out of his pocket. "See, the mark isn't so obvious now." He said, rubbing it along the car. "If you get back in, I'll guide you out."

She made a mental note of the soft South African accent and obediently closed the door and pulled forward following the instructions of the handsome male in front of the car. For the first time in years, the four friends and partners were at a party with other people instead of the usual intimate dinner together, except, Carrie never had a partner, preferring to keep her lovers away from the endless questions and scrutiny of her friends. Wow, so this is what they'd been missing all these years she thought to herself as she finally parked.

He walked to the car and opened the driver's door stepping aside.

"Happy New Year," he said smiling.

"Not quite, it's only nine thirty," Carrie responded uncharacteristically flustered, as she eyed him up and down in the dark searching for a pen and paper in her handbag.

"What are you doing?"

She was scribbling something down on the paper and looked up at him intently. "I'm writing my name and phone number of course!" she responded, tucking it behind the windscreen wiper.

"I like a person with integrity."

They were walking along the garden path following a trail of tea lights that lit the way. "I'm Ben by the way. He said, turning to Carrie. "Friend of Suzie and John." "Hi, I'm Carrie. This is the first New Year's Eve that I've spent at a house party for eh, let me see, about 5 years." "So, are you a hermit? Or a wild party animal with a preference to get wasted in an exciting city rather than a sedate country house party?"

Their footsteps crackled against the crisp frosted ground that glistened against a blanket of white, illuminated by the full moon.

"Neither," replied Carrie, her breath blew a plume of mist into the freezing night. "I usually spend it with the same group of friends every New Year, but we just decided to do something different that's all."

As they approached the festooned front door, a cacophony of raised voices and music blasted into the night indicating the party was in full swing.

"Wow! I can see I've been missing things over the years," Carrie said, excited at the prospect of dancing to some good music. She looked round only to see him laughing together with a beautiful blonde woman who clearly had her eye on him. Not surprising, given that he is probably the best-looking guy at the party she thought, looking up at the galleried stairway that was littered with people laughing, drinks in hand.

She slipped off her coat to reveal a simple gold halter neck mini dress, its loose shimmering layers skimmed her slim body to just above the knee showing perfectly toned legs down to her elegant heels. Simple and effortlessly stylish, Carrie became aware of a few heads that turned to check her out in more detail.

"Finally! Where have you been?" Rachel said, running up to Carrie glass of champagne in hand. "I'm sure you've got a bloke somewhere that we don't know about! What have you been doing?" She continued laughing. Marcus stood behind her glaring.

"I hope you haven't been drinking Rachel," Carrie reprimanded lightly, taking the glass off her, looking steadily at Marcus.

"No way hose'! This is just elderflower presse! I am just high on love!! Aren't I darling?" she said, turning to Marcus.

Carrie took a sip and handed it back ignoring her comment. "Come on then, show me the bar!"

They weaved in and out of the throngs of people until they reached the kitchen and Marcus grabbed Carrie's arm. "You look amazing," he whispered as she shook him off and poured herself a drink.

"Stop it, Marcus! I don't think I can keep doing this you know. Go and be with Rachel, she needs you." She forced herself to smile as the guilt of the day seeped inside her.

"Carrie! As usual you've out done us all again, how do you do it? You look amazing hun," Hattie said gushing. As much as she tried, Hattie had never been able to look elegant let alone trendy. For a change her unruly red hair was slicked behind her ears, and she was wearing a token slither of lipstick, but in her usual way had opted for "safe" rather than daring. The black jersey dress fell just below the knee, showing the line of extra unwanted fat around her waist, accompanied by flat pumps and black tights. A long gold pendant was the only concession to bling along with red painted nails.

Carrie squeezed her affectionately and gulped down the fizz that was in her glass. "That's better," she said topping it up quickly in an effort to relax, knowing that Marcus was watching her closely.

Jenna sidled up to the group slightly drunk. "There are a few hot guys here tonight girls," she said, looking around.

"Well, we're off limits matey, eh except Carrie of course" forgetting that Jenna's husband Jack was now out of the picture, Rachel said. She glanced over to Marcus, knowing that her husband would also fall into the category of "hot" by most women. His six-foot two frame towered over her slight five foot three inches and whilst there was a certain ruggedness about him, there was also a vulnerability that could be seen in his eyes, and something that all the women she knew loved about him.

Hattie downed her glass in one and threw her head back laughing. "Well, I'm not off limits, my husband might be here physically, but I think his head's been elsewhere for months!" Rob, who had been away three nights out of seven that week, glanced over from across the room at Hattie intuitively. Their ten-year marriage was going through a sticky patch but nothing too major as far as he was concerned. The pressure of kids, mortgage, career, and all the other things that creep into your life were beginning to take their toll. No matter, it was New Year's Eve and time to start afresh. He caught Hattie's eye and smiled, trying to mask the ripple of discontent and stop it from becoming a tsunami.

Unusually a slight tension hung over the four friends for the first time as private anxieties and secrets enveloped them in a momentary quagmire of introspection. It was eleven forty-five and people were becoming acutely aware of the lead up to midnight as bottles were passed round to get ready to toast the New Year.

"What's everyone's New Year resolution then?" Jenna said, lightening the mood. Each year for as long as they had shared New Year's Eve together, they had each confided in each other with a personal resolution for the coming year. Carrie, Rachel and Hattie looked at each other unwilling to play ball this time.

"Come on! I'll start then," Jenna said, ignoring the reluctance of the other three. "Next year, I am going to declare myself bankrupt!"

The friends turned in shock and looked at Jenna whose flushed face and quivering mouth indicated that she was telling the truth.

"OMG Jenna, we had no idea! Why what's happened? We thought your business was doing well" Carrie reacted first with shock.

Jenna shrugged her shoulders, shaking her head wearily. "I wish Cass, I wish. I don't want to talk about it now, but I'll tell you all about it soon."

Rachel put her arms around Jenna and hugged her. "OK, my resolution is that my baby is going to go full term," she said glassy eyed.

The friends looked at each other knowingly with an inherent understanding that this had to happen, anything else was unthinkable.

Hattie linked arms for solidarity. "Well, I'm not sure what my resolution is yet, but what I will say, is that my life will change next year! I'm not sure how but hand on heart, things are going to change". The cryptic message filtered across to each of them in their own way. They knew that Hattie wasn't happy at home but the safe, predictability of her life didn't echo her personality. This was something new, the flickering of a flame that was beginning to get brighter and more vibrant.

Carrie topped up their glasses and breathed deeply. "Next year is decision time for me. No more hedging my bets, no more uncertainty about my future, no more sitting on the fence." She was known for her ephemeral relationships and vagueness between the group and so no-one asked her to explain, that was pure Carrie.

The friends looked at each other and laughed with genuine affection. "All for one, and one for all!" they chinked glasses.

Three, two, one! The sounds of Big Ben on the TV rang loud and clear as the New Year came in. Suddenly a flurry of activity took over the kitchen as people turned and hugged, kissed and celebrated in unison.

Carrie looked around only to see Hattie and Rachel greet their husbands and others in the room. But the momentary pang of loneliness stopped suddenly as she felt a hand gently go around her waist and the warmth of breath on the back of her neck. "Happy New Year" he whispered into her ear. She turned and stared at Ben's smiling face as he bent down and kissed her slowly.

Marcus caught her eye from across the room and mouthed "Alright?" He was leaning against the wall, hands in pocket and had watched the whole thing holding back his jealousy. This was not supposed to happen he considered; Cass and he were mates. In fact, "mates" were different from friends, weren't they? Mates meant you could have a laugh; you could chat about nothing for hours; you could even have arguments, but it wouldn't really matter - "forever mates", everybody knew they had something special, that jokey banter that no-one else could keep up with.

Their pact to meet on New Year's Eve began five fateful years before when an innocent drunken kiss in the garden, turned into impromptu lust that seemed to have lifted the lid of his underlying feelings for her.

He remembered the moment, just after the sex when he held her face in his hands and smothered her with kisses as their latent feelings for each other surfaced and they laughingly talked about doing the same next year, with neither expecting it to happen, how could it, after all his wife was one of Cass's best friends. That moment was never spoken of again, until the end of the following December of course.

Who initiated it was of no importance, conveniently forgotten – another tactic used to abate the guilt and live the pretence of their daily lives? After several flirtatious texts with Cass, they met on the last day of the year for dinner. Of course, it wasn't just dinner though was it, he knew how he wanted things to go and persuading her that it was possible just once a year wasn't as hard as he thought it might be, considering she was a criminal lawyer, he touched his designer stubble with a rueful smile. More lies. And with lies, consequences follow, a ripple effect that took no heed of his naivety that he could love two women at the same time.

Their guilt was managed by strict agreement that they had no individual contact with each other until New Year's Eve. They would never discuss their feelings, or their mutual friends, and they would never fall in love of course. Five years on and things were more complicated now as Marcus's feelings for Carrie had deepened. He knew that she had had a few boyfriends over the years, his wife Rachel had filled him in on the sordid details, but he had never seen her with anybody else, but seeing her in the arms of a six-foot Adonis was not easy. Just a few hours before he had to stop himself from telling her he loved her because he knew that he would be breaking the rules and there was every chance their secret liaison would stop.

He took the last swig from the beer in his hands and looked away. "Come on, darling, fancy going? I'm wacked," Rachel said, breaking his thoughts as she put her arms round his waist and leaned her cheek against his chest. "Yeh, sure," he replied good naturedly taking his wife's hand and putting it to his lips. The dissipating party goers indicated the lateness of the hour as a small group of die-hards sat laughing and talking quietly together on the large grey squashy sofa dominating the lounge.

The sticky parquet flooring and party poppers strewn around were the last remnants of celebrations and the year that was left behind. Carrie and the others had already left sharing a taxi as there wasn't enough room for all of them. So, this was a sign of the new way he thought, "Me and Rachel left on our own. New Year, new beginnings" as they tumbled into the cab holding hands.

Chapter 3

January

Hattie

Hattie looked at the calendar hung haphazardly on the kitchen wall and straightened it. For as long as she could remember the family calendar had reflected the chaos in her life; always skewed so that it was slightly off centre, full of appointments with no breathing space for anyone, against a background of tired photos, school letters and bills that had to be paid. She drew a line through the first week of May and wrote Paris in capital letters across the week with a degree of satisfaction. This year was going to be different. She could feel it in her bones. Suddenly with an air of determinism she removed the paraphernalia around it, threw out the irrelevant paperwork and stood back with a smile.

The Paris school trip was something that she had wanted to do for years but had always felt that she couldn't leave Rob and the kids. Now the thought of indulging her students and herself in the art of the Louvre, Versailles and the other sights of Paris filled her with excitement, and a feeling of freedom that she had left behind years before. She had almost forgotten the art student inside her that had once loved spontaneity and hated responsibility like yin and yang.

Rob walked into the kitchen and started to make a coffee. It was one of those rare times when he had four consecutive days off and he had finally relaxed back into the routine of being at home. "What are you doing?" he said, turning to Hattie, curious to see his wife tidying up uncharacteristically.

"Just getting myself organised," she responded lightly, taking the cup that was being handed to her.

Rob took a moment and looked at Hattie. He loved the safety net of their marriage, the predictability, and the routine of their life. Some people might have called it hum drum perhaps, but for him it meant security. As a police officer he was often called away on assignments and was never able to discuss his work with her. He fleetingly recalled when they met again years after university, when he was called to Hattie's school because of an incident, and he noticed her walking along the corridor with a pile of paperwork that she dropped as she accidently bumped into him. The chance meeting rekindled a lost weekend spent in bed together after a student party.

"What?"
He hesitated before speaking, "We're alright, aren't we Hat?" he said, searching her face for a sign.
She smiled and kissed him lightly on the cheek, "Yes of course we are," she said, walking out of the room and closing the door gently behind her.

Carrie

Carrie was stressed. Only two weeks into the New Year and already she was feeling the pressure of taking on an additional client and the work that would ensue, because of her agreeing to represent Thabo Mwansa, on what she knew would end up being pro-bono work. In contrast to her personal life, professionally Carrie was always one for doing the right thing. Her inner social conscience resurfaced once again like a buoy that refused to be kept down in a pool of mindfulness, an attempt at vicarious atonement.

She knew that her boss at work was sceptical of her being successful with the case but the firm's policy on taking on one legal aid case a year meant that Carrie's insistence and passionate argument had won the head over heart argument.

She sighed inwardly and closed her eyes. The hum of the plane reverberated through her as she flicked through the film choices again trying to take her mind off the niggling thought that had hung over her since the party on New Year's Eve.

That kiss was subliminal, ravishing, sexy, and completely out of the blue, and what the hell did Ben whatever his name was think he was doing anyway she mused, as her emotions wavered from lust to irritation, and then confusion.

She thought back to his dark green eyes and dark blonde wavy hair that seemed to just touch his collar – interesting, he must be in the creative industries and not in a straight desk job she contemplated.

She was not in the habit of kissing strangers but somehow, he had caught her off guard, she was slightly drunk, and of course it was New Year's Eve, surely everybody kisses people they do not know on New

Year's Eve she thought, trying to convince herself it was harmless. So why is it that she felt cheated when he had turned and gone almost as soon as he arrived? No sooner had they pulled away from each other, breathless, an unspoken understanding between them, had somebody tugged his arm laughing as he shrugged and winked at her mouthing, "I'll be back."

Hiding her disappointment, she nodded smiling as the moment passed, and then left, almost as suddenly as it had begun.

***

The plane coasted smoothly into Johannesburg airport landing with a slight bump as it touched the warm terra-firma of South Africa. Carrie walked into the blinding sunlight and put on her sunglasses hoping that her client would not notice the bags under her eyes. Her phone bleeped a number of times as a string of texts came through one after the other.

"For God's sake! Can't anyone go off grid for a few hours without people going into panic mode!" she sighed quietly to herself glancing down at the ten messages that had been sent during the night. All of them except for one were from work, the unknown number intrigued her as she quickly swiped it open, waiting in the line for passport control. 'Hi, I understand you scraped my car and broke my side light on NYE at Suzie's party. Thanks for leaving your number, could we meet to go through details, insurance?'

Carrie had completely forgotten about the prang with the black mini parked in the driveway that night. She breathed deeply and texted back quickly, 'Hi, yes, sure. I'm in SA for work at the moment but back next week, any good?'

'Yeh, fine. Can you do Starbucks in Chancery Lane? 10am Friday?' The text came back quickly.

Of all the places, how convenient is that she wondered, knowing exactly where that was as it was close to the chambers where she worked. 'OK, 10am Friday,' she responded.

'Thanks, see you there.'

Carrie continued to the exit preoccupied with the case she was working on. It never occurred to her to ask the name of the sender or how they might recognise each other.

Jenna

"If karma does exist, it's got a fantastic PR machine. We all know the story: karma is running a great big ledger in the sky where every good deed done by every human being is recorded and at some later stage – the time to be of karma's choosing (karma is cagey that way and always plays its cards close to its chest) – Karma will repay that good deed. Maybe even with interest." ("The Woman Who Stole my Life" – Marion Keys)

Jenna had her feet curled up on the sofa trying to read her book for the next girls' night in, pondering the meaning behind the paragraph. She had done good things in her life, but were they truly selfless, perhaps she hadn't done enough. Or perhaps Karma was still waiting for the right time to repay any good deeds she had carried out in the past. What she did know was that she could seriously do with some good Karma coming her way soon.

The coffee table was a disarray of paperwork, receipts and files that could not be ignored in the run up to the annual tax return that was looming before her. In an effort to calm down and get some respite from the stress that was surfacing like a dark cloud above her, all-consuming, and seeping through like porous blotting paper, she gulped the last drop of wine left in the glass and looked around the room. It didn't take an expert to work out that her expenses exceeded the meagre income she had made during the year, she had eaten into all her savings and there was no money left to pay for her tax bill, and she had several debts outstanding. Whether it was naivety, displaced optimism that things would work out, or just plain stupidity, she had unwittingly invested more and more into the business without seeing a return on investment. The bank had called her in for a meeting and she had just managed to secure a payment holiday of three months on the mortgage, but she knew that she was in trouble big time.

There was a thud on the ceiling coming from one of the boy's rooms upstairs. She waited for more sounds; head tilted as she listened attentively. Her boys were her saving grace and what kept her going, but equally the responsibility of keeping the house and putting food on the table was weighing heavily on her shoulders. Since the split between Jack and her, she had to admit that life had been a struggle.

There was nothing untoward in their relationship, just a gradual growing apart and differing interests that eventually led to the decision to go their separate ways. The amicable split meant that he was around if she needed him, but she was too proud to turn to him and let him know that the garden landscaping business he always felt wasn't sustainable, had in fact led to her considering bankruptcy.

Her phone bleeped signalling a text. 'How are you? All OK at home? Thought I'd wish you and the boys HNY.' Jack's message came through loud and clear and for a moment she missed his smile and strong arms around her. It had only been a year, but it seemed a lifetime ago that he had occupied her bed and they had shared a life together.

He had no idea of the trouble she was in and if he did, there was every possibility he would lose all respect for her and insist on the boys living with him. His job in the city meant that he earned more money in a day than Jenna did in a month, and he could so easily step in, but pride and embarrassment was stopping her from telling him. She turned the phone off playing for time, thinking that she would respond tomorrow after a carefully crafted response.

Chapter 4

February

Rachel

Rachel hugged her knees as she sat in the warm bath brimming with bubbles and foam with mixed emotions that wavered from excitement to anxiety about the six-week scan she was due to have later that morning. As much as she wanted to see the small spec of life inside her, she also did not want to face disappointment and heartache that she had experienced so many times before. What if the fluttering inside her stomach was nothing to do with the pregnancy but something more sinister? She touched her belly and breathed deeply, "it will be fine," she told herself again and again.

She was meeting Marcus in the hospital car park in an hour. Trying not to feel affronted that he had not taken the trouble to come home so that they could go together. She pushed the negative thought out of her head and got herself ready, wishing she could officially wear maternity clothes. She looked at herself in the mirror and turned herself sideways to see if she had put on any weight at all. There was a slight curve of her belly, but she knew that this was most likely to be post-Christmas weight gain.

In contrast to her friends, Rachel was happy to be a 'stay at home' housewife even though she had a degree and qualified as an art historian such that in her early post student days she had worked in an art gallery in Brighton for two years. It was then, when Marcus Welbeck peered into the small gallery window that displayed a modern art piece by a local up and coming artist that her life changed.

She noticed the handsome face looking intently at the art and caught his eye for a split second when she smiled warmly. Never one for missing an opportunity to chat up an attractive woman, he was instantly drawn in and stepped into the minimalist white space of Haven Arts a well-respected art gallery in the North Lanes, where Brighton's most prestigious and eclectic shops were based.

She was twenty-five then and it wasn't long after a three-month romance that they tied the knot in the Surrey countryside church near to Rachel's family home. Her traditional middle-class parents were delighted that their only daughter had found someone who was financially secure and able to "keep" their daughter in the life that she was accustomed to, much to the dismay of Carrie, Jenna and Hattie who all believed that she was too young to get married and give up her career.

Marcus being five years older was, by then, a full-time property developer and had made some serious cash during the property boom in the nineties. Moving to London was a "strategic" move he said when they left the small flat in Brighton's Lanes and moved to London because that was where money was to be made. This left Rachel jobless and hapless as they hadn't taken into consideration the competition for jobs in the Capital. After six months of half-hearted applications, Rachel turned her attention to another project and worked on persuading Marcus it was time to start a family. But six months had somehow turned to six years and endless trips to the fertility clinic which had resulted in pain and disappointment that had begun to gnaw at Marcus making him feel inadequate and despondent. Oblivious to his discontent and low self-esteem, Rachel continued in her bubble of home maker and supportive wife as she unwittingly took for granted the large house, two cars, and frequent holidays, funded by his property business. She pulled into the busy hospital car park and looked around for the maternity unit with excitement and trepidation.

Marcus was early. His site meeting had ended earlier than expected because he had a cash flow problem, and the builders had not been paid. Still waiting for the sale of a property he had just developed, he was beginning to feel the pinch as the market was slowing down, and prices had begun the slow descent towards negative equity. He punched the number for cappuccino in the coffee machine and sat down on a blue scuffed plastic chair, trying to push his business anxieties to the back of his mind and focus on the next stressful thing that was dominating his life.

The impending baby scan was stressing him out. He had just come to terms with not being able to have children and was beginning to like the idea of having the freedom to do what he wanted, when bang! Rachel was in the club. In fact, what did that even mean he asked himself; parent club, baby club, life's ended club, proper adult club, once in you can't get out club? It seemed as if whatever "club" they might be joining, it was an exclusive membership only open to those who had undergone the initiation of parenthood. The uncertainty of it all troubled him, and then to top it all was this niggling longing to see Carrie again.

"Hi darling, OK?" Rachel stooped giving him a kiss. He turned towards her and smiled. "Rachel Welbeck" a uniformed nurse said looking around to no-one in particular. "Come on, that's us." Marcus said, rising and taking his wife's hands. "Let's see what the future holds," he said, squeezing her gently. They walked through to the consultation room with butterflies in their stomachs but for different reasons. The nurse checked Rachel's medical notes as she got on top of the consulting bench and lifted her t-shirt.

"OK, let's see what we have here," the nurse smiled, spreading gel on to Rachel's stomach glancing at the monitor. The murky picture revealed a blur of grey and black as the nurse moved the pen across searching, her face expressionless as she concentrated on the job in hand. Rachel pressed Marcus's hand holding her breath in anticipation. "Ah oh my!" The nurse exclaimed, turning to look at Rachel. "There's a strong heartbeat Mrs Welbeck, but you need to know that you're carrying twins." Relief, shock, and joy erupted through Rachel without warning as she burst into tears and hugged Marcus not believing that the dream she had cherished for so long, was now a reality and blessed with a ready-made family of two.

Rachel

I hold my secret close to my chest and silently pray that all is well. Please don't let my deceit lead to bad karma. I did it for the right reasons for both of us.

"Are you sure you are happy to go ahead Mrs Welbeck?" I do not hesitate. "Yes! Yes, of course". "What about your husband?" the IVF consultant asks. I tell him that Marcus is happy to give this one last go. The fact that it isn't his sperm doesn't matter, I think. I choose to omit that he doesn't know, after all, it may not be successful. I cross my fingers under the table, a throw back to childhood. It's a safety net so that I am not struck down for doing something that I know is wrong.

***

I am back in the maternity unit waiting for Marcus. The fluttering in my stomach returns. Bubbles bursting float round, pop, pop, pop.

Why am I alone again? Marcus should be with me, but here I am waiting in the hospital and he is not. Is this karma coming back to bite me? Thank goodness he is here at last. His hand feels clammy as he gently pulls me up from my seat. My secret is our future which I will keep close to me, to secure my happiness. Little do I know that it will also be my insurance policy that will protect me later in my marriage.

Carrie

Carrie sat in Starbucks, looking at her phone. The busy café was occupied by office workers using the space for meetings, laptops open, diligently texting and looking at twitter. A group text had just come through from Rachel 'Hi guys, just checking that we're all on for the next girls' night on Saturday. BTW have big news!! Just had the scan and we're having twins!! Can't believe it, ecstatic!! X.'

Before she had the chance to register the news, she was aware of somebody pulling a chair out across the table, she glanced up preoccupied, as the unfamiliar clear green eyes of Ben smiled back. Barely recognisable, his grey hoody topped a pair of dark blue tracksuit bottoms and trainers.

His dark blonde hair hung limply in soft damp strands framing his tanned face and strong jaw line. He sat down and smiled. "Hi". Carrie too taken aback by the unforeseen curved ball that had been thrown into her day, found herself temporarily lost for words. "Hi, what are you doing here?" she said cautiously, taking in his dazzling features again, now noticing his straight white teeth and firm jaw in the dappled sunlight. "Carrie, is it ok to call you that? It's my car that you smashed into on New Years' Eve."

"What? Sorry?" She had forgotten the light South African accent, still trying to register the information he had just given. He repeated himself. "It was my car. I sent you the text to sort it out." She interjected quickly before he had the chance to explain further, "Well why the hell didn't you tell me on New Year's Eve?!"

"I'm sorry. I should have. I don't know why, but I had this feeling that I'd like to get to know you better and then you wrote your number and left it on my windscreen and I kind of thought you might just want to do the business there and then, you know. I guess I would have said something to you later that evening but never got the chance." He said, sitting back as he sipped the cappuccino in his hand. He caught her eye and smiled encouragingly.

"Come on, I could have ruined New Year's Eve for you."

"How do you know you didn't?" Carrie quipped, beginning to relax. Neither of them mentioned the midnight kiss, not wanting to embarrass the other, or themselves for that matter. "In fact, why did you want to meet here? Did you know I work near here?"

"You must have been more drunk than you realised, don't you remember telling me?" Her mind a complete blank, Carrie tried to recall the evening. He went on, "As it happens, I was working around here this week anyway."

"Oh, what do you do?" Carrie hated asking that question as if it should define who you are as a person, but she was intrigued. Nevertheless, her principles outweighed her curiosity and she immediately took back the question. "Really you don't need to explain," she said hesitating, slightly embarrassed.

She need not have worried, he ignored her and looked at his watch. "I have to go I'm afraid, I just wondered if

55

I could buy you dinner? To make up for not being up-front with you?"

"What about the insurance?"

"Well, we haven't sorted that out either, so perhaps we could do that as well."

Carrie was uncertain. She didn't like the way he had not been straight with her and was still in a dark mood over the text from Rachel. It wasn't the fact that she was having twins, but more about knowing that her "arrangement" with Marcus had taken on a different level. Never did she think that feelings of loyalty and betrayal could sit side by side, fighting equally, for attention. "I'm not sure about dinner" she replied a little too quickly.

"No worries. How about a breakfast meeting? I know tomorrow's Saturday, but I could do eh, 9am?" Before she had a chance to consider the change of plan, he continued, "Do you run? I usually do an early morning run at the weekend. If you're up to it, we could go for a quick one and then do breakfast?"

The unconventional invitation threw her as she struggled to put words together into a coherent sentence. What was it about this man that made her so uncharacteristically tongue-tied? Carrie enjoyed running and exercised regularly, what harm would a quick run round the park do she thought. At least they wouldn't need to spend any time talking to each other. She didn't have the energy or head space to put forward an alternative suggestion.

"OK, Battersea Park?" She said flippantly not really caring whether it was convenient for him, and, forgetting that she was the offender in this instance. He smiled graciously, "Sure. I'll meet you at the pagoda at 9am, listen I have to go, sorry." He said as they walked to the door together and turned in opposite directions, leaving Carrie wondering what she had just agreed to and how did he know the park so well?

***

Saturday morning was blustery and cold. Carrie looked out at the grey sky and wondered why she had agreed to going out for a run when all they needed to do was exchange insurance details. Maybe she was losing the plot she wondered, pulling on her leggings. Esteemed human rights lawyer (ha ha) persuaded to do something so incongruous to her usual way without the slightest attempt to assert herself and disagree. She shut the heavy black door pulling it closed with the brass knocker, typical of the double fronted Victorian houses that were a few streets away from London's famous Battersea Park.

What if he wasn't there? What if he was there and had no intention of going for a run but just doing it for a joke? She felt slightly foolish and began to doubt her decision as she cautiously approached the pagoda in the middle of the park looking around. The park was quiet probably because of the inclement weather with few people around. There seemed to be no sign of Ben. Carrie began to question her stupidity when from behind he appeared in tracksuit bottoms and tee-shirt showing signs of wear with a slogan that said 'You read my T-shirt. That's enough social interaction for today.' The wet patches under the arms and his damp hair indicated that he had already done some exercise, "Hi, sorry you've had to wait, I've just done a quick circuit as I got here early. Shall we get going?"

"Sure," Carrie responded and started running ahead. He caught up quickly and continued at her pace.

"So, do you run here often?"

"I didn't realise South Africans were so cheesy," she said, breathing heavily as her breath melted into the mist that was enveloping the park in a grey blanket of obscurity. "Sorry if I'm not posh enough for you, but that's a fairly obvious question if you're running with someone," he said under his breath.

"What? I'm not posh."

"OK." The indifferent reaction implicit in his belief that she was.

"What makes you think I'm posh anyway?" Carrie persisted.

"I thought you said you're not posh."

"I'm not!" she retorted quickly.

"Other than you have a posh accent, posh job and posh friends," he said under his breath.

"What?"

"Nothing"

They had run about 3 kilometres and were slowing down to jogging pace into the wind. Rain had started to fall bouncing droplets off their faces. "You're soaked," Carrie said looking at the drop of water hanging off Ben's nose. "You're posh," he said running faster. "No, I'm not!" she said, tugging his arm. "Ok, I bet your flat has loads of books, furniture from Laura Ashley and a small TV." Carrie hesitated for a moment wanting to correct him but realised that he was right on all counts. "I don't have lots of books and it happens that I have a small flat, so the TV isn't that big."

"OK," he said unconvinced. They had left the park and were walking side by side along Battersea's residential streets with cars parked bumper to bumper. Ben didn't know where they were going but he was happy to continue walking along as long as he still had her company. Carrie's black front door came into sight, its brass door knocker gleamed invitingly against a window box of winter pansies and crisp architectural planting. "I suppose you'd better come in so that I can sort out the insurance details. Do you want a coffee?"

She disappeared to change leaving him to survey the surroundings of the neat ground floor apartment. Wall to wall books in the two alcoves framed a Victorian fireplace and large mirror cleverly placed to reflect the small garden outside. The cream sofa and armchairs faced the fire and various pieces of art collected from Carrie's travels formed a diverse and colourful collection of photographs, and abstract modern art against the white facing wall. No TV he noted smiling, but a large CD and vinyl collection. If it wasn't for the uncleared empty wine glass left on the floor next to a large Afghan floor cushion, she might be thought to be a bit "up herself" he mused, looking at the several personal development books on the bookshelf.

Carrie walked in with her hair in ringlets. She had managed to get in the shower for five minutes to warm up and strolled into the room in a pair of fluffy socks, track suit bottoms and casual hoody. "OMG, I'm so sorry," she said, apologising to Ben as she noticed he was wringing wet. "I'll get you a towel to dry off."

"No worries. I've got a change of clothes in the car. I'm only down the road so if it's ok with you, I'll go and get them and change here if that's ok?" he said, walking to the front door. There was a slight awkwardness between them now that there was nothing left to do but talk and sort out the insurance details. He came back within a few minutes and disappeared into Carrie's study to put on some dry clothes. The proximity of the study with its half-opened door could not help, but draw her eye, to the gap that revealed the tight torso and tanned six pack of Ben as he pulled on a fresh T shirt. She poured the coffee into two mugs diverting her gaze to the back door that opened on to a small patio.

They sat at the breakfast bar in the modern kitchen with their arms just brushing against each other, sending an electrical shock through Carrie. She adjusted her posture and tried moving her chair slightly so that she was more facing towards him. As much as she was dying to find out more about him, his lack of forwardness and laconic speech brought out her shyness, such that she quietly waited for him to lead the conversation as she busied herself finding paper and pen to write down her insurers.

The momentary silence was broken when he laughingly described the trials and tribulations of being a professional personal trainer and body coach for several high-profile clients across London. Down to earth and with an honesty and refreshing transparency that Carrie had not come across for years, his humorous anecdotes about certain clients resulted in laughter to the point their stomachs hurt. She wiped the tears of laughter from her eyes and glanced down at her watch, it was 1 o'clock. "Do you want to go out to get something to eat? There's a great little bistro around the corner," she said, knowing that she was taking the lead.

It was dusk by the time they left the cosy restaurant. A large carafe of wine later they emerged from the fug and noise of weekend lunchtime revelry into the cold winter air. Carrie knew she was slightly drunk but in a good way. For once she had let her hair down and showed the side of her that only Marcus truly had seen. Fresh faced, minimal make-up, and as she had accidently left her phone at home, no mobile to distract her. Ben therefore received her undivided attention as she lapped up his charming accent with anecdotes that continued to keep her laughing the whole afternoon. She felt as if she had been cocooned in an exclusive bubble for hours and found herself wanting more. They walked back to the apartment unspeaking in comfortable silence.

"OK, I'll be in touch about the insurance then," he said, looking at her. "You did give the details to me, didn't you?" he said, putting his hands in his jacket to check but finding no trace of paper.

Carrie knew she had written it down but now, not so sure that she had given it to him. "I did write it down I know I did," she said, beginning to laugh. "You are a human rights lawyer, right?" he said, chin down, eyes up. "Yes, of course, and I know it is your human right to get compensated. I'm sorry," she continued laughing. "I'll go and get it. I think I left the paper in the kitchen."

He started to laugh with her until they both held each other for support. He looked at her momentarily and wiped a tear from her eye "I've got to go. Text me the details." Not sure if she was expecting a kiss, Carrie abruptly sobered up. "Yeh, sure. Thanks for today, even if we didn't get the insurance sorted out."

"No worries," he smiled and kissed her lightly on the cheek as he headed down the road to the tube leaving his car in situ.

Carrie let herself into the dark apartment and turned on a side light. Her mobile confirmed it was seven o'clock and a group chat text – next get together Friday at Rachel's 7pm.

Chapter 5

March

<u>Hattie</u>

"She studied her husband. He turned his body to the left and right, almost pacing on the spot, highly agitated as if warming up for a run. His eyes darted to the clock and the window, as if he had a place to be. Rosie would have found it difficult to describe him to anyone that didn't know him as she did. But it was as if he was already a stranger. She felt no more able to touch him, hold him, kiss him than any man on the street, and at that realisation, she felt the beginnings of fear"
("My Husband's Wife" – Amanda Prowse)

Hattie went slightly cold as Jenna read the paragraph out and remarked, "Don't you think that's so evocative? I can so imagine what that's like. I know that Jack and I separated, and it was nothing like that but the idea of somebody who you've loved becoming a complete stranger would be terrible wouldn't it?"

"I can relate to that," Hattie said quietly, looking into her glass.

The four friends sat around the oak farmhouse table in Rachel's kitchen as Jenna watched Hattie spin the stem of the wine glass round with her fingers repeatedly. She exchanged glances with the others before continuing. "Why would you say that, Hattie? Rob's lovely".

"I'm not talking about Rob. I'm talking about me."

"huh?"

Hattie sighed and looked up. Her face pale and lined, looked strained. "I'm the one, not Rob" she paused to see what reaction was occurring across the table. No-one revealed their thoughts, as they each waited for further explanation. "I'm the one who's become the stranger, not Rob. I can't explain it, but I feel as if I've lost sight of who I am, who I was. Sometimes I catch sight of myself in the mirror and don't recognise the person I've turned into."

Jenna thought back to their student days recalling a tall lean figure with wild flame red hair and corkscrew curls who was always late for everything. Her talent for painting and drawing gave her gifted status at Art School where her final exhibition was highly acclaimed, and she had begun to get a few commissions. Hattie's eclectic and diverse interests gained her the nick name of PP short for pied piper because of the ever-increasing number of people she seemed to collect. She would often turn up at parties with new friends or put people together by connecting different people she had met and who she thought would get on. Then Rob came on the scene. Serene, steady Rob who was the antithesis of Hattie. He was her yang to her yin or that's how she described him to the rest of the group after a weekend of spontaneous lust.

They met at a party one evening in the middle of December just as the run up to Christmas partying had started. Rob was sitting in the corner of the room getting quietly drunk as he watched an amazing woman making a spectacle of herself on the dance floor. She had an ethereal quality about her as she spun around laughing in a world of her own somewhat oblivious to the other people dancing. It was a Friday night and he had nothing better to do than be at the party held by one of his flat mates in their shared house. Being a maths student, he was not in the habit of mixing with flamboyant art students; a pint in the Student Union bar with a small group of mates was more his thing but he felt safe and invisible in the corner of this crowded room, slowly being by this woman who was clearly off her head.

Hattie's head was spinning. She stopped dancing and watched the room continue to swirl in a flurry of lights and faces. If she wasn't going to sit down deliberately then there was every chance that her body would have willed itself on to the floor, anyway, acting as if it had a mind of its own. She took the decision to sit down and found herself a dark corner occupied by a very straight guy but through the haze of alcohol also looked quite interesting. Hattie liked "interesting". She preferred interesting to handsome as she peered at him closely.

"Hey, do you mind," Rob said, moving over to give her some space. "Sorry but do you know anybody here? I just wondered what connection you have to the party, it's just that I haven't seen you around". She said, speaking slowly and deliberately in an effort to put a coherent sentence together. "It's my house." Rob replied without offering any further explanation. "Huh?" Hattie responded confused. Unravelling what he meant was far too complicated for a very drunk art student who preferred visuals to conversation. She decided to pursue another tack and took his hand, looking at it closely. Rob, unused to such spontaneity and intimacy allowed her to examine his long, tapered fingers finding the gesture slightly arousing. "Nice hands" she murmured.

"Thanks".

She was on a roll now. The alcohol had stimulated her senses and love of people, she wanted to find out more about this person sitting next to her, who seemed to be a guest at his own party. It turned out that they were polar opposites; she loved art, he liked science; she was extrovert, he was introvert; he liked rock music, she loved pop; she hated exercise, he loved and played sport; he was a man's man, she loved women; she loved books, he never read anything and so it went on. Hattie had never met anybody with such a different point of reference to her and found this fascinating. Equally, she was so of another world to that of Rob's, she was constantly drawn to a place in his heart and mind that he would never have ventured into without her. She didn't remember much about how they ended up in his room, but they woke up the next day with legs tangled around each other and stayed there for the rest of the weekend, venturing out for cups of tea, food and then more alcohol.

"What's happened to me people?" Hattie said rhetorically.

"Life. Hattie. Life's what's happened," Carrie said, studying Hattie's face for a sign that might reveal her feelings further. "You've got two lovely kids, a husband who loves you, a steady job teaching" a lot of people would say that you're pretty lucky".

"But who am I, Cass? Am I Hattie the mum, Hattie the wife, Hattie the schoolteacher? I seemed to have lost sight of who I was before kids, before Rob, before teaching. She paused, gathering her thoughts, "Look at me, for God's sake, I'm over-weight, frumpy and boring!"

It was true that Hattie had never lost the pregnancy fat and had somehow never really got back into the flamboyant clothes that were her signature trademark whilst a student, but there was a tacit acceptance between the friends that this was just something that had happened to Hattie after settling down and dealing with the responsibility of having a family. "You are not frumpy or boring," Carrie said unconvincingly but feeling the need to say something.

"Yeh right," Hattie responded sarcastically. The other three caught each other's eye and looked down as the atmosphere went from warm to cool. "So, what do you want to do about it?" Jenna asked, pouring wine in everybody's glasses.

"I really don't know," she said elbows on the table, head in hands.

Chapter 6

April

Jenna

Jenna walked purposely along the high street towards Blanchets, the coffee house where she was meeting Jack for their monthly catch up. Their relationship had turned into a mutual support system for each other, although it was probably more heavily weighted towards Jenna. It wasn't a formal arrangement but more something that had evolved over the months, beginning with a casual phone call from Jack enquiring about the kids.

The suggestion of coffee in a mutually convenient place away from the home they once shared seemed like a good idea, and they met like good friends without an agenda. That was the beauty of their relationship. They met, they chatted, Jenna told a few white lies about her business, they laughed, they kissed as friends, and they returned to their separate lives until they met again.

She knew this time would be difficult though. Jack was bound to ask how things were going. Not because he was being controlling, but more out of a sense of duty, and also pure curiosity. Being a financial man, he enjoyed the financial aspects of business resulting in a seamless line of innocent questioning that made Jenna squirm every time they met.

She pushed open the door and looked around the busy café until her eye fell on the familiar figure of her estranged husband. He sat reading The Guardian in a quiet corner engrossed in the sports page. His salt and pepper hair had grown longer than Jenna had seen for a long time as she noted the designer shirt and faded straight legged jeans. The thought crossed her mind that he had lost a few pounds and looked a bit younger, but she couldn't quite place exactly what was different about him, or perhaps he had always been like that, but she hadn't noticed. She hadn't bothered putting on any make up or had barely put a comb through her hair and had begun to feel self- conscious in front of her neatly turned-out husband. The feeling was unfamiliar as she had never cared that much about how Jack saw her, but now for some reason, she felt acutely aware of his eyes looking at her as she walked towards him.

"Hi," he said, smiling and getting up. "I'll get the drinks." She sat down slightly breathless from walking and removed the scarf around her neck that was beginning to feel stifling, at least she'd have time to compose herself.

"How's it going?" Jack said, placing two cappuccinos down. "Fine," Jenna responded on automatic pilot. She was used to saying "fine" to everything these days when asked. "And the boys? How's Jo getting on at school? Andrew seems pretty sorted for uni in September it seems." He continued pressing whilst making light conversation.

Jenna seized the opportunity to talk about the boys and relaxed as she spoke about her favourite subject, filling Jack in on all the details of school, sports activities, and the usual sibling arguments that surfaced over the last few weeks. He listened intently, watching her closely. Her eyes seemed to flit around the room and avoided his whilst she spent an unusually long time stirring the coffee slowly. When the coffee was finished, she diverted her attention to twirling a strand of hair finally running out of things to say. "So how are things with you? How's work?" she said, reaching into her bag to check her phone.

He sat back relaxed. "Pretty good actually. I have a new boss as it happens." She looked up at him curiously "Oh. What's he like?"

"He's a she actually and she seems great. She's only been in post three weeks but so far so good."
"Is that why you've let your hair grow and lost weight?" Jenna asked trying not to sound bitchy. As usual Jack didn't take the bait and smiled. "I'm glad you've noticed; got back into the football and just laid off the carbs for a bit that's all". Their eyes met fleetingly "It looks like you've lost a bit too" he continued. "Really?" She shuffled uncomfortably in her seat.

"How's business?"
"Come on Jack don't start on that again. Do you know how annoying it is when you constantly ask me about MY business which you are not part of!"
He persisted, ignoring her irritation, "Have you had many commissions? I'm interested Jen that's all."
She shrugged her shoulders huffily, "Yes I have actually! In fact, my diary's pretty full," she said lying.
"Really?" he responded, raising his eyebrows.

Jenna's landscaping business and her wish to set up on her own came from a series of constant whines from her when they were still together. Flexible working so that she'd be around for the boys, being her own boss, being able to earn more money echoed in his ears. She had always loved gardening and had designed their own urban oasis at home such that visitors began to ask her to help design their own gardens. Six months later with a landscaping and horticulture qualification under her belt, she gave up her job working in the city where she had met Jack and opted for a better work life balance and the ambiguous status of 'business owner'.

For somebody who trained as a financial advisor, Jenna seemed to have lost all memory of financial planning and good judgement as she began to invest heavily in design services, a bespoke website, marketing brochures and other set up costs. Fuelled by one or two enquiries that didn't lead to sales, she continued to take on small jobs for friends and under-priced her services when quoting. The amicable separation came when Jack suggested he moved out to give her more space to run the business, taking advantage of an opportunity to avoid the all-consuming hobby cum business that was slowly dominating their lives.

"Yes. Everything is good." Jenna reiterated again.

"How are you managing cash flow Jenna?" he questioned, looking at her steadily.

"Jack, I don't need to explain any of my business to you," she said tight lipped.

"Well, I'm afraid it is my business Jen if our house is in question."

"What do you mean?" she asked nervously.

"Jen, I've heard from the bank" He said exasperated. They sent a letter to me confirming the 3-month payment holiday."

The bombshell that Jack knew she was in trouble came without warning. Stupidly she had not considered that as joint mortgage holders the bank of course, would write to Jack as well as her. Still not able to come to terms with the reality of the situation she shook her head smiling, "Honestly Jack, it's really not that bad."

Rachel

Rachel sat up in bed perfectly still, frozen to the spot. She didn't feel right, something wasn't right, she just knew it. She touched the slight round of her stomach lightly and felt for movement; nothing, not a flutter or the slightest indication that there was a life growing inside her. Her skin hot and clammy made her thighs stick together forcing her to prise them apart slowly with rising panic that the bedsheets felt damp.

Breathing slowly, she took in deep breaths through her nose and out of her mouth just as she had been shown by the nurse when she succumbed to panic attacks. One, two, three she continued breathing in and out, eventually forcing herself to peel back the duvet to see if she was bleeding.

She opened her legs and looked down as her mind played games and fear turned to confusion. The crisp white sheet continued to hold the secrets of the night without giving anything away, its pristine brilliance refusing to reflect her anxiety. She reached over to the bedside table and picked up her mobile and dialled Marcus.

The phone bleeped in Marcus's trouser pocket intermittently. He ignored it and tried to concentrate on listening to what he was being told by the architect and site manager. The distracting signal meant that only certain words made it through to his consciousness, subliminally infiltrating the seriousness of the situation he was facing. "So, the upshot of all of this is that we are 6 weeks behind schedule, and we can't go any further until we get planning permission for the extension and you're estimating at least twenty grand more than originally budgeted?" he reiterated, making sure that he had heard correctly whilst trying to do the maths in his head.

The project was the most ambitious he had undertaken in the ten years he had been property developing, and he was certain when he first found the property, that he would make a killing, but now he wasn't so sure. Endless problems arising from unforeseen damp, weak foundations, and ancient beams, in the listed building meant that it was soaking up money into the ether. He had run out of money and unless he got a lifeline soon, he wasn't sure how he was going to resolve things. The phone bleeped again forcing him to check it with a degree of irritation. 'Call me asap, it's urgent!' the text read in capital letters. Three voice messages and two missed calls. Marcus cut the meeting short and phoned Rachel as his anxiety levels heightened in the anticipation of more bad news.

"Are you bleeding?" he questioned her ignoring the crying.
"No!" she wailed back.
"What?"

She calmed down enough to talk "I just don't feel right."

"Why don't you feel right? Has something happened?"

"No not as such, it's just that I can't feel anything."

"Babe, it's probably nothing. I can't come right now but I'll take you to the hospital this afternoon, OK?"

"Why didn't you pick up when I called?" she asked sniffing.

Rachel's neediness was beginning to wear him down; he breathed deeply, "Rachel, I was in the middle of a site meeting. I had five people here who I'm paying by the hour and there's... Oh, never mind." He knew she didn't want to know his excuses.

***

The dark London streets gave a false impression of the hour as one could be mis-led into believing that it was far later than five o'clock. With few words spoken between them since leaving the hospital, Marcus was trying to control his irritation and understand his wife's level of anxiety around the pregnancy. So, she was still pregnant, and there was nothing wrong, he said to himself. All this fuss and paranoia and she's fine! She has nothing to do each day, no responsibilities apart from herself, and still, she's not able to deal with "stuff" alone.

They came to a standstill as the traffic lights turned red, Rachel looked across to Marcus and touched his arm, "OK?" He tried hard to loosen the tightness in his face and smiled falsely, "Yes fine" he said lying.

"Is something wrong darling? Tell me, I'll understand" she said feeling an atmosphere forming. She knew he was pissed off with her for making such a fuss and calling him so many times before she'd even investigated things properly.

Marcus couldn't stop himself from retorting "That's just it Rachel. You think you understand but you don't! You don't want to understand. All you want is to flit around in your own special world that has no place in the reality that everybody else lives in." He said heatedly.

"That's not true."
"Really? What exactly do you think I do every day?"
"Don't be silly, darling. You're a property developer. You have to visit properties and check that everything is being carried out to your specifications."

"Yeh, that's all I do," he said, shaking his head and pulling off as the lights changed. "Never mind the financing, negotiating with banks, managing the people, juggling ten different things at once, trying to be in three different places at the same time."

"That's called multi-tasking darling women do it all the time." As soon as Rachel had made the flippant comment, she knew she had stepped over the line.
Stoney faced, Marcus drove home and swung the car into the drive aggressively turning off the engine. "Don't patronise me Rachel," he said quietly fuming. "What do you know about multi-tasking huh? What, putting the washing on whilst making a cup of coffee? When was the last time you properly worked? What was it, six years ago?"

"And whose fault was that?" She didn't wait for an answer and continued, "You were the one who insisted on moving from Brighton! I had a job. I had a career. It was only when we moved here that things changed."

"So, it's my fault then? I seem to remember that you were the one who chose to give up looking for a job and concentrate on having a baby! Why you thought that you couldn't work and do both like most women is beyond me!"

"What? You did want me to work?" she said incredulously.

"What do you do exactly each day, Rachel?"

"I keep myself busy. You'd be surprised at what goes into managing the house."

"Surprise me."

"Now you're just being obtuse," she said, opening the door, knowing that the argument wasn't going anywhere.

He followed her into the house carrying his anger inside him as he purposely threw his jacket in a heap on the floor knowing that the gesture would wind her up. Rachel held back the tears and went upstairs for a bath, frightened that the stress would affect the lives growing inside her.

Marcus took the opportunity to open a beer, taking satisfaction from the gauge he left on the bespoke wooden work top as he opened the bottle, using the edge to knock off the top. He took a swig and downed half its contents in one gulp and reached for his phone. Breaking the rules, he found Carrie's number and texted, "Hi Cass, I know it's against the rules, but I need to talk. Any chance?"

'No soz. You know the state of play. It won't help things. Stick to the rules.' Carrie pressed the button hastily as her emotions heightened reading the text. Marcus needed a friendly ear but if they were to continue, he had to keep to the plan. Tough love Carrie called it. She knew that he would understand, let's face it, they were playing a game of cat and mouse, that was the fun of it wasn't it? she told herself, as she turned her attention to the impending South Africa trial.

The dim light in the candlelit bathroom brought a certain tranquillity to Rachel as she lay in the bath, trying to forget the exchange of words she had just had with Marcus. Suddenly the bleep of her phone signalling a message jolted her out of sleepiness, as she opened the cryptic text from Carrie. She quickly texted back. 'Not sure who that was meant for but want to know more! Next girly night then? ☺ Xxx'.

Chapter 7

May

A Man with two houses loses his mind. A man with two women loses his soul – Chinese proverb

Carrie

"Marriage had seemed natural to them. They talked about it. If you find the right person, and you are both sure, then you can't be too young, can you?" And even at twenty-four both of them had felt too old for the sad dance of the gym and the bar and the club". ("My Favourite Wife" – Tony Parsons)

Carrie got in late and frantically tidied up the flat. Thank God for home delivery. Three late work nights in a row had had their toll, as washing had piled up, and ready meals had taken over from the usual healthy food option. How she had agreed to host the girls' night at her flat was beyond her – she knew that the text had come through when she was mega busy, and so she agreed in haste, to avoid the merry-go-round and tediousness of endless, group messages.

With just enough time to pull on tracksuit bottoms, she pulled her hair into an untidy knot, and began to relax as she gulped half a glass of wine down, trying to ignore the dichotomous thoughts that swayed her thinking. Spend time with her closest friends, or run as far away as possible?

Laughter and voices outside her window signalled that the peace inside her flat would be disrupted within moments. She opened the door, and the three friends tumbled in gaily throwing coats and jackets on the coat stand, slipping off shoes in the way that is never questioned with the closest of friends.

"Come on then Cass, where are the glasses? Let's sort out priorities!" Hattie said, following Carrie into the kitchen. "OK steady on. I've only just got in," she responded with two bottles of wine in hand. The four friends hadn't seen each other for weeks and even texts had been intermittent as their lives had begun to tell a different story to what they were telling each other.

"What's going on then?" Jenna said, sitting on the floor asking the question to no-one in particular.

"Has anyone actually read this month's book?" Carrie asked hoping to steer the conversation away from personal news. "OK, let's just get that out of the way quick then," Rachel said laughing. "Yes, all read it I think" she said looking round for confirmation. They all nodded in unison, "As it happens, I thought it was one of the best books I've read in a long time" Rachel interjected. "It kind of reminded me of me and Marcus. You know, the way the characters met, and marriage was just the right thing to do."

"Yes, but then look what happened," Jenna said. "He ended up being besotted by another woman, didn't he? So much for the perfect marriage. But I know you and Marcus aren't like that hun."

"Oh, don't be so sure Jen," Rachel said slowly, wishing that she was on the alcohol like the rest of them.

"Well, the only similarity that I see is that you got married at the same age, twenty-four."

"Were you only twenty-four?" Jenna said, thinking back to the wedding. "It's so young when you think about it but then you were both so sure that it was the right thing to do."

"Well, it was at the time."

"Why do I get the feeling there is a "but" coming along?" Carrie asked before she could stop herself. Marcus had never discussed his relationship with Carrie, and she had never asked, but the recent text he'd sent to her had a tone of desperation about it, and she couldn't help but feel that all was not right.

"When we first met, he swept me off my feet remember? And then things seemed to move pretty quickly. We basically slept at each other's flat every night from the day we first met. I think it just seemed natural to get married." The rosy glow of the past had dimmed Rachel's memory as the insistence and pressure of her domineering mother had got into her psyche, and wedding plans seemed to take over without any pause for thought.

"Oh, I thought that your mum and dad put pressure on Marcus to do the right thing?" Hattie reacted trying not to provoke Rachel.

"That's right! Jenna exclaimed nodding her head, "Weren't your parents keen to get you settled?"

Rachel's parents were an old-fashioned pair who somehow always acted and appeared older than their age. At the age of 30 her mother was already of the mindset that she was too old to wear certain clothes, style her hair in a particular fashion, or go out socialising. She was content to stay at home and look after her much loved daughter who was cosseted to the point of obsession. When the time came to leave home and go to university, happiness replaced anxiety that their only child was making her way in the world without them. Settling down with a reliable husband was surely the best thing for her and the longing for a grandchild may have turned dreams into reality had Rachel been able to conceive.

Rachel, always loyal, shook her head, "No they were really happy for me and Marcus, but we decided on our own." She said forgetting the heated discussion she'd had with Marcus after a visit to her parents, when they had both pressurized her to find out what his intentions were.

"Yeah, but I remember you didn't want to give up your job, did you?" Jenna persisted. "No, of course I didn't want to give up my job! I didn't stop working because I got married, it was because we moved away from Brighton!" she exclaimed heatedly.

Rachel didn't like this new focus on her and Marcus and wasn't quite sure how the conversation had turned towards her. Usually, one for keeping her relationship secrets to herself, she was beginning to feel an uneasy sense of disloyalty to him and wished she hadn't said anything.

The others exchanged glances just as Rachel looked up to catch Carrie's eye. She wasn't enjoying the attention on her and took the opportunity to divert things. "So, who's your guilty pleasure then Cass? Spill the beans."

The random comment hit Carrie like a bolt as she flushed momentarily processing the rhetoric. "What?"

"You know, the text you sent to me, something about sticking to the rules, what rules? Remember? I'm assuming it was meant for someone else. You're such a dark horse Cass, so come on, tell us."

Carrie recalled the day that the Thabo Mwansa case had hit the news in South Africa, and she had been in back-to-back meetings all day. The day of the text from Marcus asking about meeting him - it had come through as she was walking from the office and into another meeting. The familiar muffled ping in her handbag notifying her of a text.

As if on automatic pilot she glanced at the text and responded without even thinking. For five years they had continued this secret liaison and had kept the guilt at bay by having no contact with each other, a mutually convenient arrangement, that whilst on the wrong side of her moral compass, she had managed to bury because of the burden and responsibility of her work. For three hundred and sixty-four days a year she deliberately chose not to think about it and then for one day she would allow herself to let go – she calculated that it was zero-point twenty seven percent, a negligible amount of time in the scheme of things, her barrister training convincing her that it was allowed, as fact took over emotion.

The cryptic comment from Rachel made her heart sink as she realised that she had accidently sent her response to the wrong person.

For the second time that night, the four friends realised that their lives were taking different paths, and regardless of the intimacy of their friendship, some things might never cross the threshold and enter the domain of the four friends. It struck her that sometimes what we want and what we fear can be distinguished by the blink of an eye.

Hattie

The clothes pile that resembled a jumbled mass of colour and textures spilled across the kitchen table as lace, cotton and silk lay in an incongruous mountain of organised chaos. The bib of her faded dungarees hung loosely to hide the layer of extra fat around her stomach, protected by the blue and white tie-dyed vest that revealed the small dark tattoo of yin and yang at the top of her left shoulder, a throwback to her student days whilst travelling with the group in Kenya. Despite the tight fit, the outfit suited her character – off the wall, bohemian, and unconventional in the sense that nothing quite matched, but there was nevertheless an effortless ensemble of styles that reflected Hattie's artistic nature. Her red wavy hair was pulled high into an untidy knot and her fringe kept off her face with a floral bandeau reminiscent of a 1950s maid.

Unused to ironing, with a preference to shaking wet clothes thoroughly to remove creases, this was a novelty for Hattie as she took a cerise coloured silk top off the pile and started ironing it carefully trying to curb her excitement. The school trip to Paris was less than a week away and she had for reasons unbeknown to her, decided to ransack her wardrobe and pack clothes that she hadn't worn in years.

"What are you doing?" Rob questioned incredulously, walking into the kitchen and seeing the chaos. He looked at his wife wearing dungarees that he had never seen before. "What are you wearing?" She chose to dismiss any reason to defend what she was wearing, and instead looked up smiling brightly. "I'm getting ready for Paris darling, remember? I'm off on Friday, aren't I?"

"But you never iron! What's with the sudden frenzy of activity?"

"Rob, I'm representing the school and leading a group of sixth formers. I have to make sure that I look professional and appropriate. Anyway, why shouldn't I iron if I feel like it? I can get more into my case if it's all neat and flat," she continued.

Trying to work out the rationale behind her explanation was beyond Rob; whether she would fit any of the clothes she hadn't worn for years, never mind the fact that they were neither professional nor appropriate by all accounts was not worth arguing about. He smiled inwardly as he caught a glimpse of the woman, he fell in love with at that party all those years ago.

***

"The Mona Lisa has an enduring appeal," Hattie said, looking at the painting intently with her group of students. The small group gathered round listening as she continued to enthral them with her passion. "See, if you look carefully, you can see that her eyes follow you wherever you are standing. Da Vinci's use of optical effects makes her smile enigmatic, almost as if she is looking through each one of us, almost mocking, don't you think?"

"Well, I don't see it myself. Personally, I have always felt that this painting is over-rated. Leonardo as an artist as so many paintings that deserve just as much if not more analysis" a soft, tinkly, French accent came from the edge of the group. Hattie looked up and followed the voice until her eye fell upon a striking woman with short auburn hair and wide green eyes and high cheek bones. Her porcelain skin was offset by dark red lips that formed a beguiling smile, reaching the creases of her eyes. She leant against the wall with her arms folded and legs crossed, her head slightly tilted as if waiting for a response.

"Sorry?"
"I said that I think this painting is over-rated compared to the other fantastique works by Da Vinci."

"Well, that's down to personal opinion, and of course all art is subjective," Hattie said above the heads of the group who were exchanging glances and nudging each other. The woman smiled and nodded her head in concession as Hattie fleetingly caught her eye before moving the group on.

It was eleven o'clock in the evening when their paths crossed again. Feeling a sense of claustrophobia from the small cheap hotel Hattie felt the urge for some air and left the warmth of the building in exchange for the cold, sharp air and bright lights of the Tour Eiffel that shone on to the pavement outside the hotel. She wrapped her scarf around her stuffing her hands into her pockets for warmth. There was a slight breeze that brought the temperature down with its wind chill. With no particular direction in mind, she looked around and walked through the hotel's best feature, the garden that led to the entrance of the building.

"Salut," a soft voice whispered in the dark. Hattie turned to see the woman from the Louvre sitting at a table smoking a cigarette. "Hello again," she said, stopping to acknowledge her properly, noticing the espresso cup on the table as she casually leaned on her elbow blowing smoke into the dark night.

"I am sorry if I appeared rude this afternoon. It's just that so many people fail to look at all the other wonderful work that Da Vinci painted don't you think?" she smiled.

"Not at all, everyone is entitled to their opinion, and anyway I agree with you. I'm planning on taking my students to see less obvious works tomorrow."

"La belle fronnierre is worth comparing if you haven't already considered that," she said, holding out her hand "I'm Francoise Besier, by the way."

"Hattie." The formality of the French was something that she still hadn't got used to, "Hattie Stewart" she reiterated taking her hand and shaking it lightly. It felt cold with long fingers and rings on four slim fingers. "Enchante," Francoise responded squeezing her hand in acknowledgement. "Please," she said, gesturing to Hattie to sit down. "Eh, I'm sorry I was just thinking of going for a stroll."

"Oh, yes c'est froid n'est pas?" she said, falling in and out of English as she got up. "May I join you? There is a small bar at the end of the road, if you would like to get out of the cold?" The idea of going somewhere warm and having a drink appealed, it had been a long day. "Sure, why not?" Hattie said as they walked side by side towards the entrance trying to not feel in awe of the stylish woman next to her. She could not help but notice the tight jeans tucked into knee high biker boots and dark green suede coat belted tightly to accentuate a slim waist. "What brings you to Paris?" she said, turning to Hattie. "I'm on a school trip - sixth form art history A-level and you?" Hattie asked.

They approached the small café and walked into the warmth to find a cosy table near the window obscured by frosted glass. "Sorry, you asked about me? Like you, I am also here for a short trip, I'm in education too as it happens," she said, smiling warmly as she loosened her scarf. Hattie took a gulp of wine larger than she intended, and felt the colour rise from her neck up to her cheeks. Hearing that this new-found colleague was a Professor of Art History at Cambridge University had brought back latent feelings of inadequacy. She glanced down at her vibrant orange woollen jumper and dark green jeans thinking that the striking woman opposite most probably likened her to a proverbial English carrot. Her hair let loose formed a mane of rust as its unruly ringlets cascaded down to her shoulders.

"You seem, anxious, are you OK?" Francoise said quietly, looking at Hattie. The quiet astuteness of the observation went through her like a knife, she hesitated before speaking, "Sorry, for some reason and I'm not sure why, but I feel a bit in awe of you," she said with typical candour. Francoise threw her head back and laughed. "Well, there is absolutely no need to feel that way! I'm sorry, I shouldn't have, how you say it, rained on your parade this afternoon. I appreciate your honesty. Come, let's have another drink, shall we? I feel I'd like to get to know you."

They ordered a second carafe of wine and finally Hattie began to relax. "So why did you infiltrate my study group?"

"Like the Mona Lisa, your eyes drew me to you."
Francoise said, winking mischievously.

Jenna

Jenna drove along the leafy suburb of Hampstead singing loudly along as Taylor Swift's album Red played on the car stereo, an album she put on whenever she was in a feel-good mood. Finally, business had picked up and the latest commission from a wealthy client in Hampstead Garden Suburb, her first proper project for months, had lifted her spirits. The first sign that the long winter months were over had come through as dappled sunlight filtered through the leafy roads casting intermittent shadows along the rows of spring daffodils. "Today is a perfect day. Like hipsters aha aha... I don't know about you, I'm feeling twenty two.. aha aha..." The banal lyrics were perfect for a car sing along as Jenna turned into the driveway of the large, detached property set back from the road.

The gravel drive crunched under the tyres as she turned the music down and slowed down to take in the garden at the front, noticing a walled perimeter with a wooden gate that appeared to lead to a second garden that circled the rest of the house. She slammed the door shut and walked to the austere black front door with the garden plans under her arm.

"Mrs Timpson?" she said, extending her hand to the stylish and immaculately turned-out woman standing in the doorway. Her slim, elegant frame was set off by a woollen violet and pink plaid skirt and sugar pink cashmere sweater. She ignored the gesture and stepped aside to allow Jenna to enter the wide lobby, with its parquet floor and antique side table and fresh lilies, carefully placed in a round glass bowl.

"Please come in." The clipped public-school accent gave no warmth in its tone, making Jenna immediately wary as she stepped inside the hall where sunlight shone through the stained glass to the side of the lobby. "I take it these are the plans," she remarked as she led Jenna through to the orangery at the back of the house. "Yes, I've drawn up the plans for you to approve. Hopefully, we'll be able to start work on the garden shortly," Jenna said, noticing a fluttering in her stomach, and wondering why she didn't feel more confident. She knew that her design was good, but she had never had a project of this size before and felt daunted by the officious woman who was beginning to show signs of being a nightmare client.

Desperate for a coffee Jenna hoped that the offer of one might come her way. Instead, she found herself spreading the white art paper on to the oak table whilst carefully observing her client's facial expression and pale blue eyes. The soft pastel watercolours of the design were a profusion of pink, violet, yellow and blue hues carefully coordinated in deep sweeping beds. Steppingstones had been carefully designed on the lawn to lead to a stone water feature and fairy reminiscent of a Hans Christian Anderson tale – depicting the sartorial elegance of a quintessential English country garden.

Sarah Timpson stared at the detail closely as she put her designer glasses on to inspect the drawing that whilst beautifully drawn, had no resemblance to the conversation she recalled having at the first consultation meeting. "What's happened to the ethereal, bohemian style we discussed?"

Jenna processed the remark before responding "Mrs Timpson, the entire design is based on an ethereal quality of being in another world, hence the fairy steps that lead to the fountain and the delicate choice of colours." She remembered taking notes of the conversation and whilst she knew and understood the meaning of ethereal, she deliberately checked its meaning before she began planning.

"Well, it's not very bohemian. I wanted bohemian!" the client said petulantly.

"Bohemian and ethereal are two very different things Mrs Timpson."

"No, I'm afraid they are not! I was expecting something like Yves St Laurent's Garden in Marrakesh, not some twee English country garden!"

The fact that Jenna's client did not know the meaning of ethereal or bohemian was neither here nor there. From Jenna's point of view, she was in a no-win situation. She had already spent a week drawing up the plans, and plants were waiting for collection from the nursery. This would mean a complete revision of the whole design and would require cancelling the plants for which she had already put down a deposit.

She realised that she should have spent more time on finding out more of what her client had in mind, perhaps looking at colours and photos of things she liked, but her inexperience prevailed as she enthusiastically lapped up Sarah Timpson's ambitions and luxury budget.

"I'm sorry but it's not what I wanted. I'm afraid you'll need to go back to the drawing board; and I'd like to see the revised design by next week as this has put things back by a week and I have an early summer party planned."

The conversation reminded Jenna of teacher pupil dialogue where the teacher did all the talking and the pupil got rapped on the knuckles. She bristled at the reprimand and rolled up the drawing slowly making an effort to blink away the tears that were on the brink of making her look unprofessional. "That's fine Mrs Timpson. I'll go through colours and tone and then send some images to you before the design is drawn up again." She knew that the redrafting was going to cost time and money that would affect her already unstable financial situation. Sarah Timpson opened the front door and smiled falsely with her lips pursed.

Jenna, relieved to get into the safety of her car and drive around the corner, quickly pulled into a nearby parking space hidden from the property. The humiliation of the morning swept through her, as the tears that she had held back came flooding through as if a torrent unleashed through the opening of a dam.

Chapter 8

June

Rachel

Marcus feels distant and aloof. I feel distant and aloof. I am not interested in his work, I have bigger things to care about, bigger responsibilities, but he doesn't seem to see that. My job of keeping my babies alive is more important than whether planning permission is given for a building. I cannot do housework; I need to keep still as much as possible. I feel safe at home, I do not need to go out I tell myself and try and persuade Carrie to come here. Instead, we reach an agreement for the coffee shop nearby.

I can't find a coat that fits. Everything is too tight now, but I manage to squeeze into something and keep the buttons undone. My anxiety takes over and I forget where I have left my bag, how on earth can I go out? Perhaps I'll phone and call it off. I have forgotten how to behave in public, it's so long since I've been out; I feel as if I'm in a bubble looking out on to a world that I don't belong to. I am worried about my marriage – why doesn't Marcus seem interested in me? Why doesn't he seem interested in our pregnancy?

I try not to think about other possibilities, after all my priority is keeping my babies alive. But still, the thoughts continue to seep into my brain. Pictures of Marcus in my head. He's with somebody but not me. Who is he with?

Now I realise that his physical presence remains, but his mind left me a long time ago.

***

Café Nero was busy that morning Rachel noted looking around. It was the first time she had left home in more than a week and now that she was out of the safety of her house, she felt weird, almost an observer to a world that she did not belong to.

A clique of Mums who had gathered with their toddlers for a chat and a coffee, suited women and men with laptops quietly surfacing the net and looking at emails, and older grandmothers stopping for a rest with what could be their daughters. She did not belong to any of them; she sipped the coffee slowly feeling sorry for herself and checked her phone again for the time, beginning to feel irritated at being kept waiting.

Carrie pushed the door open twenty minutes later, breathless from running from the car park. It was a rare day when her diary allowed her to work from home in the morning and she had agreed to meet Rachel on her way to the office. The cryptic text asking for a chat had put her on edge slightly as she avoided a one-to-one situation with her as much as possible, preferring to always see her along with the rest of the gang.

"Finally," Rachel said, smiling to hide her frustration. "Sorry. I had a phone meeting before I left, and it went on longer than expected." Carrie flopped down on the sofa opposite throwing her suit jacket on the spare seat. Speaking to anybody outside her immediate circle of friends and Marcus was beyond the boundaries that Rachel was used to. These days her world was so small she barely spoke to anybody.

A slight awkwardness hung over the two friends as they adjusted to the unusual situation. "How are you? Everything OK?" Carrie asked casually. "Not really. Marcus is wrapped up in a world of his own. He's totally consumed by work and never seems to have any time or interest in what I've been doing."

"What have you been doing?"

"Well, not a great deal but that's not the point, is it? He's just not showing any interest in the pregnancy or anything else for that matter!" The high-pitched reaction reverberated across the room as an elderly woman looked up and exchanged glances with her middle-aged daughter sitting opposite.

"Steady," Carrie said in a low voice. "He's under a lot of pressure with his business, isn't he? It's pretty stressful managing projects when money's involved."

"How would you know?"

"I'm guessing," Carrie said, feeling uncomfortable. She hadn't spoken to Marcus, but she knew from the limited time they spent together on New Year's Eve that his business was almost at the point of make or break.

"Why are you defending him?"

"I'm not defending him Rachel. It's just that, well let's face it, you don't work, and I think you've forgotten what it's like to have those pressures. I know that you have also had the pressure and stress of trying for a baby over the years but it's all good now isn't it? You're carrying two healthy twins which is fantastic. Why don't you just enjoy it and indulge yourself? I'm sure Marcus is just trying his best to support you by bringing in the money."

"Well, that's just it. He isn't bringing in the money. He's always complaining about how much I spend and how much expense he has with the business. I don't think he wants us to go away this year. You'd think that this year especially before the twins arrive, he'd want to go away."

Carrie remembered the text she received from Marcus and felt a pang of regret and guilt for not supporting him. Hearing one of her dearest friends' whine like a spoilt child was bad enough but she imagined that if Rachel continued in this way at home it would just drive Marcus away even more. She wanted to empathise but increasingly Rachel's need for attention contrasted vibrantly against her client; unjustly incarcerated in South Africa, and patiently relying on his faith in humanity to give him the freedom he had lost through no fault of his own. "How do you want things to change Rachel? Is there anything you could do to help improve things?"

Rachel had never considered that she also had responsibility to change things. Taken aback she struggled to comprehend the question. "I do my best," she replied quietly.

"I know you do. But what does that mean Rachel? If you're keeping the house tidy, making sure Marcus has a nice meal in the evening and being someone who he can talk to and you still think he's not happy then maybe you need to re-think what doing your best means." Carrie knew she was pushing the boundaries but none of their friends had had the nerve to approach the subject with her.

"What would you do? For somebody whose never had a relationship beyond 6 months you can talk the talk."
"I know and I'm sorry, probably the lawyer in me," she said shrugging without hint of upset.

Despite her petulance, Carrie knew Rachel had a good heart. The guilt she felt crept into her head once again as she looked affectionately at her friend wearing her signature Boden wardrobe but now in maternity mode.

Rachel sat back and stared across to Carrie as their eyes met. "I know!" she exclaimed. "Why don't you have a word with him? You two have always been close and I know that you'd be able to find out what's going on." The ingenious plan was set in Rachel's mind as she continued excitedly, finally finding a solution to getting Marcus to open up. "Why don't we organise a drink in the pub one evening but then I pull out at the last minute."

Carrie could not believe how things had turned. If they had been playing a game of chess, she would now be in check mate if she didn't think of a way out of this soon. "Eh, I'm not sure Rachel, I have a lot of work on at the moment," she said, playing for time.

"You always have a lot of work Cass. Nothing new there. Surely you can help out your oldest mate. I wouldn't ask if I didn't have to."

"Well, don't you think Marcus would think it odd?" Carrie questioned knowing the answer.

"No of course not! He'd probably think it weirder that I wanted to go out."

"Exactly!"

"Cass, please? I know he'll talk to you and at least you can then let me know if you suspect anything."

"What do you mean suspect anything? Suspect what?"

"I don't know. I've probably been reading too many trashy magazines. I'm just worried that's all."

Carrie knew she was digging a hole for herself which was getting bigger by the minute. "OK," she agreed reluctantly, secretly planning to bail out at the last minute.

Carrie

"What I know for sure is that every day brings in a chance for you to draw in a breath, kick off your shoes, and step out and dance – to live free of regret and filled with as much joy, fun and laughter as you can stand. You can either waltz boldly on to the stage of life and live the way your spirit is nudging you to, or you can sit quietly by the wall, receding into the shadows of fear and self-doubt" ("What I Know for Sure" – Oprah Winfrey)

Carrie read the paragraph repeatedly as she sat in the corner of the bar in Battersea trying to stop herself from feeling anxious about the impending meeting with Marcus. Why was it that every book that was up for discussion with the girls, seemed to have something pertinent within the writing? This night out was breaking all the rules – she knew that Rachel was going to bow out even if Marcus didn't; now it seemed that she was caught in a web of deceit between two of her closest friends.

What was her spirit nudging her to she wondered? Did this mean she should not regret the times she'd shared with Marcus? Time that amounted to just 5 days, or if you counted the hours, most probably about two and a half days she calculated idly. The problem that Carrie had, was that kicking off her shoes and taking a leap into the unknown, had led her to touch the stars, but also step into the darkness that by its very nature brought fear, uncertainty, guilt, and doubt. Now lurking in the background was an incessant recalling of the Saturday she had spent with Ben, unplanned in its effect on her emotions, and which had left her wondering why she couldn't stop thinking about him.

Marcus walked up to the bar and ordered a beer, and glass of wine for Carrie. He saw her sitting in the dark corner shrouded by palms and felt his heart skip a beat. She had her head down and appeared to be reading a book oblivious to the drinkers sitting nearby. Her glossy hair fell in smooth folds to her shoulders, and she was bare faced. He loved the fact that she always remained true to herself, refusing to get caught up in the corporate world, and yet, she looked stunning and always commanded a double turn. He could not believe his luck when Rachel had arranged a get together for no particular reason, and then abruptly dropped out due to hormones and morning sickness. So now he was given a clear licence to have the evening with her and he couldn't wait.

He walked over, glasses in hand, "Hi Cass," he said, smiling softly at her and sliding next to her on to the bench. She moved across and kissed him lightly on the cheek with the familiarity of old friends who didn't need to try with each other. "Who'd have thought it," he said, taking a gulp of the beer and relaxing into his seat. "What do you mean?"

"Well, I wasn't expecting to have you all to myself for at least, eh let's say seven months or so".

"Marcus, stop it. I didn't actually want to do this. It doesn't seem right."

"You don't seem surprised that Rachel isn't with me?"

Carrie knew that she could not lie to him, he would see right through her, such was the connection between them. "I'm not. Rachel set this up because she wants me to find out what's going on with you. She can't work out why you're not interested in the pregnancy and she's getting paranoid that you might be wanting more than she can give, I think." The candid straight talk was of no surprise to Marcus. He loved that about her as he watched her use her hands animatedly. He didn't need to ask why Rachel had thought that Cass was the best person to talk to him; everyone knew that they were mates in a different way to the other husbands. "I just don't want to do this Marcus. I don't want to be the go-between you."

"Shall we talk about us then?" he said, downing the last of his pint.

"huh? There is no us. What are you talking about?" Carrie said a little too heatedly.

"Cass, stop trying to pretend that nothing has happened between us for fuck's sake! We've spent the last 5 New Years' Eves in bed together! You can't block it out completely, I know I can't."

Carrie put her hands through her hair and momentarily closed her eyes. The hub bub of laughter and voices resonated in the background as she tried to gather her thoughts. "Marcus, I can't do this anymore."

"I sent you a text a few weeks ago. I needed to talk. I know we've got an agreement not to speak, you know during the year, but I could have really done with somebody to talk to you. What happened? You didn't even tell me to fuck off?"

"That's because I did tell you to fuck off, but I sent it to the wrong person by mistake."

"Oh. So, who got the brunt of your anger then? Poor sod."

"It was Rachel actually. I just went on to my contacts and obviously found the wrong "Welbeck"."

"Well, why didn't you just reply straight away after I sent it to you?"

"I don't bloody know! I was thinking about things."

"You know for an international lawyer you can be pretty ditzy."

"Shut up, I was busy."

Once again, the banter started between them and Carrie relaxed realising just how much she missed him. His fingers brushed against her hand and she found that rather than recoiling, she allowed him to touch her until their fingers entwined into a natural knot. There were too many words, too many questions and too many unspoken feelings to even begin a meaningful discussion. They chose instead to lock eyes and smile, as if silencing their thoughts would remove the reality of the situation they had constructed through their own naivety and self-centredness, when they had followed their bliss five years earlier.

The large yellow full moon shone low and brightly over Chelsea Bridge. Its light illuminated the river and reflected the black glass of the sky, mirroring the modern architecture that dominated the river Thames. The unusual moonlight, seemingly evoking a magical realism, causing people to spill on to the London streets drinking and socialising in the balmy evening.

A tantalizing hint and the promise of Summer was within their grasp. Carrie and Marcus walked along Chelsea Bridge towards Carrie's apartment on the other side of the river. Marcus stuffed his hands deep into his jacket pockets to stop himself from putting his arms around her which he knew might result in a rebuke.

She on the other hand felt the warm fuzzy glow of the large wine, and oblivious to Marcus's feelings, slipped her arm into his, as she had always done with friends who she felt completely comfortable with.

They walked in peaceful silence until the breath-taking beauty of London's night skyline commanded their attention and they stopped to admire the view. Carrie leaned against the bridge to steady herself and looked across at the river. "If you could have anything in the world, what would you have?" she said turning to Marcus. It was one of those questions that is often said frivolously with an assumption that the answer would always entail more than the contentment of an individual's own reality. For Carrie though, she really did want to know what was most important to him, after all, his answer could lead the way to them deciding about their own futures.

"That's a bit random, isn't it?"

"Maybe it is."

"What would you have?" Marcus said, turning the question back on to her.

"I don't know, probably good health, a loving relationship, and a family I guess." He stood behind her and looked across to the same view, his arms moved round her waist as he nestled his face into her hair. Marcus had all three, a bullseye in fact. He realised then how lucky he was but still he couldn't stop himself. Carrie turned to face him, her eyes glistening, "It's time to stop Marcus."

"I know." And then they kissed with a passion that put the whole evening into a spin of irrelevance.

Chapter 9

July

Jenna

Jenna followed the Manager of the care home trying to put a lid on the guilt she was feeling as she carefully avoided looking at the frail residents who sat together in the communal lounge. Despite her reluctance, her peripheral vision found its way to an elderly woman sitting by a window looking out to the garden beyond. She felt compelled to turn sideways to look at her properly noticing the lines on her worn face and her almost snowy white hair combed neatly into a bun to the nape of her neck. Her pale blue cardigan was neatly buttoned to reveal a cream collar belonging to the blouse beneath. Her knees were covered by a cream blanket, but her expressionless face masked the secrets of her thoughts and chequered history that took her as a refugee from Poland to England as a child.

Clare Brannigan the Irish care manager stopped and touched Jenna's arm lightly. "Come on, I'll get you a cup of tea," she said in a soft Dublin accent. "How much independence do the residents have?" Jenna asked still looking at the woman by the window. "Oh, they can have as much as they want or need. Doris over there, she's ninety-two you know. She came here almost six years ago, and she was so active when she first arrived, but she just loves looking at the garden now."

They walked to a small office near the bright reception area as Jenna relaxed and began to properly take in the surroundings. Floral curtains, brightly painted walls, bookshelves stacked with large print books and games, and piped music in the background. It was a bit like a hotel for elderly people she found herself thinking, that can't be so bad. "Could you let me know how much care costs here for permanent residents?" "Here is the brochure but basically it's £800 a week." Jenna mentally added up the cost for a year as the figure of thirty-seven thousand pounds surfaced to her brain.

She was barely earning eight hundred pounds a month now and whilst her mother had equity in her childhood home, it would take months to sell and release the money. She had to do something quickly, but panicked thoughts clouded her judgement and thinking, as her mind raced to consider the limited options that appeared to confront her.

She drove home with the slow realisation that her get out of jail card might lie with Jack who she knew had savings and the disposable income that she had left behind ever since their amicable split. She thought back to the last time they met for coffee a few weeks ago and felt a rush of affection that she hadn't expected.

The engine purred quietly as she took stock of the situation with a mixture of emotions that fought through guilt, regret, sadness, loneliness, and helplessness. She recalled the frequency of heated exchanges with Jack over her insistence to start her own garden landscaping business and his calm, reasonable responses that now on reflection made perfect sense. And yet despite his reservations, he gave her the space and encouragement to follow her bliss but perhaps his leaving to allow her to develop the business was his way of following *his* bliss – she questioned his motives now for the first time since he had left, with the slow dawning of her own selfishness. Ashamed, she dropped the handbrake and pulled forward into the road and headed in the direction of the city and Jack's office.

Life had a habit of sliding up behind Jenna and poking her in the back whenever she found herself indulging in her own insecurities, or paradoxically when she felt completely confident and determined to do what she thought was right, regardless of everybody around her.

There was the time that she insisted on taking her mother to Spain, despite her protests and frailty, which were over-shadowed by Jenna's absolute conviction that the holiday would be good for her. The heart attack that ensued whilst in Spain was no doubt linked to the stress that the so-called holiday had created. Then there was the plan to move the boys into a fee-paying school, again a whim that seemed to be created in a dream, but which turned into reality as she convinced Jack it was the right thing to do.

A year later after bullying and drugs, they moved back to the solid-state grammar school around the corner after Jack's insistence. There were so many treasures in Jenna's life, but she had never stopped to appreciate them; now the prospect of a new dawn was beginning to emerge as she found a parking space opposite his office, her heart racing.

Twelve forty-five – he was bound to come out for lunch about now she pondered knowing that Jack was a creature of habit. If she could catch him leaving for lunch, she would treat him to lunch as a surprise. The thought excited her with a gradual dawning that she still loved him.

Checking the clock on the dash her eyes flicked across the road as she saw his familiar figure stepping out of the building. He was laughing and talking animatedly to a woman by his side. Jenna sat up abruptly and watched their interaction which seemed to imply an intimacy that was beyond work colleague friendship.

Her cream trench coat was tied tightly around a tiny waist, set off by shoulder length dark blonde hair and black heels. Although she had a youthful look she wasn't 'young' but probably a similar age to Jenna. He held the door for her as they stepped out of the building, but the telling sign was his hand that slipped with an intimacy and ease to the small of her back as he ushered her out.

Carrie

"It all began with a simple question that no-one could answer" ("Born to Run: The Hidden Tribe" – Christopher McDougall)

The simple sentence had a resonance about it ever since Carrie had first leafed through the book in the small independent book shop ahead of the next girls' night in. Back in her office she contemplated the sentence and asked herself what might be the question that no one could answer regarding Thabo Mwansa. The question being, why would a successful doctor who had struggled to get the education he deserved, throw it all away by raping a patient? Why would he? He was happily engaged, he had the highest credentials and personal qualities by all accounts, there was no track record of any aggression or misbehaviour as far back as the research showed, so why would he put himself in such an untenable position? What if the question wasn't about Thabo she wondered absentmindedly, as her thoughts transferred to an alternative scenario. Perhaps the question should be why would any patient call rape on a doctor if it were not true?

The young woman in question had no reason to falsify a story but equally, Thabo Mwansa did not seem to be rapist material – why would he jeopardise his career, his future, his finances, after such a long struggle to be qualified. He was well regarded professionally but also had earned genuine fondness and was highly thought of by people outside his professional life. Carrie sat back in her chair and closed her eyes for a moment as she tried to assemble the sequence of events as she had been told by her client.

The bleep alerting her to a text jolted her back into the room as she reached for her phone glancing down.

"Fancy a run along the tow path tonight to brush the cobwebs away? Curry and beer to put the world to rights after?" Carrie's heart leapt when she saw Ben's message. It had been three weeks since they last went out and even after the banter and laughter fuelled by alcohol, she was still uncertain about his feelings towards her.

The drunken kiss that New Year's Eve night was becoming a distant memory that had begun to take on an ephemeral quality as if it had never happened. But since then, as their friendship grew stronger, the seeds of something deeper seemed to have waned. The fact that he hadn't made a move on her at all other than a light kiss goodbye, began to chip its way through to her ever-present insecurities but equally challenge her feminist principles.

She pondered over the text wondering, while her feelings of inadequacy hovered above; why should she assume that just because they hadn't gone to bed that he wasn't interested? Her fingers quickly moved across the phone in response; "Yeh, why not. What have you been up to?" "Busy as usual; 6pm? I'll pick you up from the office?" "Sure. See you later x." Carrie hesitated over putting a x at the end of the text and reprimanded herself for being so sensitive about it, for God's sake they were friends at the very least.

**

The warm sunshine of the day gave way to the beginning of a pink sky across the London skyline. The temporary heatwave had caught many Londoners off guard as office workers spilled on to the streets to enjoy the start of the weekend ahead.

Carrie bent down to tie her laces grateful for London's melting pot of cultures and colours knowing that her shorts and neon vest would not get a backward glance in the city that she loved.

Their route started at Westminster Bridge, an iconic starting point dominated by Big Ben and the Houses of Parliament. Running at a steady pace, they continued along the tow path missing the throngs of tourists and office workers enjoying the warmth that resonated off the pavements.

Neither spoke as each took in the sights of the city and being in the presence of each other's company. Carrie felt comfortable alongside Ben, almost too comfortable she realised, as they came into view of the London Eye and headed towards the city. The buildings changed to modern glass structures that sat in equal status to traditional buildings reflecting the fabric and ethos of this iconic city – tradition and modernity side by side.

She glanced across to Ben, noticing his strong chin and tanned face, he was good looking there was no doubt about that. "You OK?" He said noticing. "Yeh, fine. London's beautiful, isn't it?" "It sure is. I love this city. Do you want to stop at the Millennium Bridge? My apartment is just over the river."

"Why not, yes ok."

They slowed down to a light jog as the bridge came into view. The Tate Modern was on the opposite side of the river, boats moved effortlessly up and down and people from all walks of life leaned against the railings taking photos of the London skyline. Carrie held on to the railings and stretched her arms out exhaling as her breath slowed down to a normal pattern.

"I needed that, thank you," she said, turning to Ben who had his back to the railings sipping from a bottle of water. "Tough week?" he said, smiling gently.

"A bit, I suppose. Nothing more than usual; it's part of the job. I feel so responsible all the time." He stood behind her and put his arms on the railings and looked at the river.

Carrie felt a thrill as she felt his body brush against hers. He leaned nearer to her face and whispered, "Come on. You need a drink." They walked side by side along the bridge and turned to a side street a few minutes away from the famous art gallery. The area once run down and derelict a decade before had been regenerated and replaced with warehouse lofts, small bars and tiny restaurants.

"Here we are," Ben said, twisting the key in the lock and kicking the door open with his foot to reveal a large airy open living space. Two squashy sofas were divided by a low coffee table with magazines, books and a coffee cup. Modern art and framed photographic prints were strategically placed on one facing exposed brick wall, two large potted palms occupied the opposing corners. The modern kitchen was in the far end of the room dividing the living and eating space by a breakfast bar and three high stools. Cream rugs and ornaments from around the world were an eclectic mix of old meets new.

Carrie walked in taking in the space and feel of the apartment. She realised then just how little she knew about Ben but also how she wanted to know more. The furnishings and objects around showed a glimpse into his world which was much more interesting than she had given him credit for. "Wow, this is beautiful" she said as he followed her in. "Yeh, I love it. Look why don't you take a shower if you want? He said opening a door and gesturing. She nodded in agreement and cautiously walked into the room that had a large antique carved bed and pristine white linen.

The modern shower room was off the bedroom. Clean, functional white tiles and black towels, quality toiletries just my kind of style Carrie thought as she stepped into the shower and began to relax as the stresses of the week washed away. She padded back quietly refreshed into the lounge and watched him from across the room as he effortlessly moved around getting glasses and beers from the fridge, unaware of her gaze.

Her eye took in the stylish interior that was an eclectic mix of modern and traditional art from South-East Asia and Africa. A series of four large black and white photographs hung on the facing wall, carefully positioned to complement each other reflecting the four seasons spring, summer, autumn and winter but not a typical weather landscape, more abstract including shots of people. "Hi, feel better?" he said across the room, but Carrie was too distracted by the handsome profile of Thabo Mwansa in shadow against the breaking of the summer dawn.

Chapter 10

August

Hattie

Hattie tied the shoelaces of her trainers and stretched. Friday evening, the best day of the week she thought as a feeling of excitement surfaced at the prospect of the weekend ahead. She stood up and smoothed down her vest, noticing that the love handles she had got used to had disappeared. She shut the chipped white painted and weather worn front door and began jogging down the residential street crammed on both sides with parked cars.

For some reason unknown to her, an epiphany had occurred since she had returned from Paris. The revelation that she was still the person she always had been, and that deep down buried under layers of stress, responsibilities, and the pressures of life, lay the remnants of her bohemian youth which had resurfaced, and now that it was out, it was hard to put it back. Three weeks and four days post Paris, she had lost 8 kilos in weight and was the lightest she had been since her student days.

She found her rhythm and made her way into the nearby park, noticing the splash of fading yellow and white summer colour in the deep flower beds that lined the route used by runners and cyclists alike, and the first signal that Summer was passing by.

Francoise's friendship had given her a new lease of life. The gentle cajoling, the wry wit and sense of humour, and the razor-sharp mind, was a breath of fresh air to Hattie, who needed a friend in her own right, outside the inner sanctum of the book group. She loved them all of course, no doubt about that, but they were all so straight and conventional she considered.

Carrie was probably the least conventional but, she was also a human rights lawyer, travelled around the world, and was spectacularly pretty. Rachel was Miss Conventional with a baby on the way and no plans to be anything but a housewife, and Jenna, well, she was just a bit mumsy, constantly worrying about her boys. So, where did that leave her? She chided herself for being so critical of her closest friends, reflecting that she was also just a boring housewife and teacher so no change there.

Her thoughts turned to the last text exchange she'd had with Francoise as a smile crossed her face thinking of the wacky photo of her dressed in gold from top to toe including gold face paint for a party that she was going to under the theme of sartorial elegance. The live photo using i-message showed her winking directly with the caption "Gold Blend, better than a cup of Nescafe."

The texts and emails had started shortly after Paris and since then the two friends exchanged news and jokes every day. Hattie's heart swelled when she thought of the weekend ahead prompted by the impromptu invitation to Cambridge and an art exhibition and opening launch given by one of Francoise's colleagues. The offer of the spare room and meeting a new group of people excited her, but at the same time was excruciatingly scary, as the familiar, safe, unconfident Hattie that she believed she was, jarred with her alter ego, and the person she really was. She glanced down to her Tracker – eight thousand steps and 6pm. She groaned inwardly to herself, honestly what does it take to do ten thousand steps people she wondered as beads of sweat trickled across her forehead.

"Hello darling." Rob called out over his shoulder as Hattie closed the door behind her and walked into the kitchen limp with exhaustion.

"Fancy a drink later? Remember I've got the weekend off." Her stomach lurched as she realised, he had forgotten that she was to be away in Cambridge for the weekend. She quickly recalculated the options in front of her: one – just say no and remind him that she had a weekend planned about to leave in an hour? Risk factor – he would go nuts and they would row. Two – go for the drink and leave in the morning. Three – cancel the weekend. Damage limitation was her best bet she considered, after all, it was rare for Rob to have a weekend off and it was sods law that she had a weekend planned at the same time.

"OK, let's go out tonight and get a babysitter, but remember I'm going to a gallery launch tomorrow in Cambridge" she said, lightly kissing him on the cheek to soften the blow as she walked past.

She texted Francoise before getting in the shower 'Soz but I'll have to come tomorrow now, hope you understand." Francoise texted back by return in her usual easy-going style. "No prob just come directly to the launch as I'm out during the day now. Anytime from 6pm x." Hattie jumped into the shower wondering what she had planned considering she was supposed to have been there with her.

**

A few heads turned when she walked into the crowded gallery space that was the venue for the exhibition of paintings by a talented new abstract painter. Whilst old Hattie had wanted to melt into the walls, new Hattie couldn't help but make a statement. Her vintage velvet jacket and silk t-shirt complemented the black leather skinny trousers and high heeled ankle boots and mane of unruly red curls that cascaded down to her shoulders. The outfit had cost her a small fortune but hardly any of her current wardrobe fitted these days, and Francoise had shown her that clothes should be an investment.

She looked around casually for her friend spotting her talking animatedly with a glass of champagne in one hand. Feeling her presence, the French woman looked up and smiled broadly, kissing her French style on both cheeks. "I knew you'd look fantastique! Come, let me introduce you to my friends" she smiled leading her to a group of people talking to the artist.

Hattie blushed. She was in awe of this hip, eclectic crowd. Where had she been all this time she wondered, feeling self-conscious. She gulped the champagne and breathed deeply allowing the alcohol to take effect. "I'm not sure if I can do this," she murmured under her breath to Francoise walking towards the group.

"Yes, you can." She smiled guiding her into the inner circle. "Sorry to interrupt everyone but I have to introduce you to my most remarkable friend, Hattie. Please look after her as she doesn't know anybody here and I have to mingle," she said, giving a tinkly laugh. Hattie looked imploringly at her glassy eyed. Francoise turned and blew a kiss with a cheeky wink as she left Hattie to talk to the group.

***

It was twelve thirty exactly when it happened. Hattie remembered it vividly even though she knew she hadn't been that drunk in years. Six glasses of champagne and a few small canopes meant that her inhibitions unfolded as the evening wore on. Somehow, she had managed to not make a complete fool of herself and found that her new-found joie de vivre was entertaining all those around her.

Finally, in the quiet surroundings of the apartment, Francoise poured the steaming coffee from the cafetiere into two small mugs and handed one over to Hattie in the modern kitchen. "It was lovely to see you so happy tonight," she said, looking across. "What?" Hattie caught her eye and looked down as she casually sipped the coffee and leaned against the dark, granite kitchen work top, feeling unnerved by her gaze. She glanced up to see Francoise smiling at her. "What? What are you smiling about?" "I'm just glad you came that's all," she said, walking over to her. And then it happened – the slow lingering kiss that started as she whispered "thank you" into Hattie's ear as she casually put her hands through the unruly curls and turned Hattie's face towards hers.

Rachel

Rachel could barely get behind the wheel of the car because of her bump. She squeezed in behind the wheel and adjusted the seat breathing heavily. Chauffeuring people around seemed to be her main job these days as everyone took advantage of the fact she was not drinking. She clicked the seatbelt into place and searched for her phone amongst the chaotic contents of her uber large Gucci tote on the passenger seat. Six months into the pregnancy she had reached the glowing period, where people remarked continuously on how she had blossomed and she herself had noticed the glow to her skin and hair. Even Marcus seemed more interested these days, well at least on the physical side of things, emotionally she still couldn't fathom what was going on in his head as work seemed to dominate as usual.

She was determined to corner Carrie this evening to find out if he had said anything to her when they went out. Over a month had passed and she hadn't heard a thing from her but she also knew that Carrie wasn't the sort of person who'd pick up the phone and have a gossip, she was too discreet for that, and let's face it she did have a mega powered job in law, although no-one actually knew exactly what she did. In fact, what was going on in Carrie's life she wondered absentmindedly, releasing the brake, and moving off. There was obviously some bloke she had been seeing who she'd met through scraping his car but beyond that was anybody's guess.

Rachel sometimes wished she had Carrie's life – wouldn't that be good she pondered. No responsibilities, lots of money and disposable income, men dropping at her feet and a figure that was the envy of everybody that crossed her path. She knew that underneath the superficial glow, Carrie's life was most probably not like that, but the more Rachel felt and looked like a beached whale, the more diminishing was her self-esteem as she considered if she had lost sight of who she really was before the bump, before London, perhaps even before Marcus.

She pulled up outside Carrie's flat and hooted the horn with no intention of getting out of the car. Inside the cosy flat Carrie knocked on the window in acknowledgement and sat back down on the sofa with her mobile to her ear trying to wrap up the conversation. "Do you know somebody called Ben Kingsley?" she repeated to Linda Mwansa via skype, frustrated with the intermittent connection and muffled sound. "Ben? Yes, he went to the same university as Thabo, they were great friends."

The horn hooted again. Carrie waved through the window and pointed to the phone shrugging in apology. She persisted, "Linda does Ben know that I'm representing Thabo?" she said, hoping that it was pure coincidence that their paths had crossed at the party. "Yes, he does. In fact, it was Ben who suggested I contact you. Why are you asking?" Carrie's heart thumped hearing the response. "I'm so sorry I have to go out now, can we speak again later this week?" she said, picking up her keys and heading for the door as they agreed to speak again in a few days.

"Don't mind me," Rachel grumbled under her breath as Carrie opened the car door and climbed in next to her. "So sorry Rachel, it was a work call which I had to take," she said with her mind racing. Her flushed cheeks caught the attention of Rachel.

"Everything alright? You seem a bit hyper."

"Yeh, goes with the territory I'm afraid," Carrie shrugged, as she tried to shake off the nagging thought that Ben knew something about the Thabo Mwansa case but wasn't letting on.

***

"It's getting late. I don't have too sharp a sense of time anymore, but I know it must be after eleven and maybe even getting on for midnight. I'm reluctant to look at my watch though – because that will only remind me of how little time I have left" ("Limitless" – Alan Glynn)

"Bloody hell! That's an opener, isn't it?" Jenna exclaimed as the rest of the group sat round the kitchen table drinking their second bottle of wine. "That's how I feel," she said, qualifying her thoughts. Since seeing Jack walk out of his office with an unknown female, she had begun to obsess over him to the point that she had gone to sleep thinking about him and often woke up imagining him lying next to her. Was it just pure jealousy and the fact that he seemed to be content with their new arrangement, or was it that she had finally come to her senses and realised what she had – only time would tell, but from her point of view time was running out?

Jack's regular calls to her had begun to get infrequent and when she had tried phoning him, he seemed to be constantly on voicemail. In fact, he had changed his voice message which is something he hadn't done for years. His quiet, deep voice sounded chirpy and more upbeat or was she imagining it. For Jenna, this was the first time in fifteen years that she felt insecure and she didn't like it. Jack had always been there for her, even when they decided to have a break to allow her to focus on her landscaping business. Now she wasn't so sure that this was the reason for his suggestion, perhaps it was just an easy way out of something that had begun to show cracks. She swallowed and smiled as confidently as she could, "I went to Jack's office to take him to lunch last week."

"Why do I think there is a "but" coming," Carrie said gently, looking at the others.

"But before I managed to call him and suggest it, I saw him walk out with a new colleague – his boss I think, and they seemed pretty close. So much so, they were laughing about something. And there was something about the way they were with each other that makes me wonder if he's found somebody else." She pursed her lips to hold the tears back.

Rachel sighed and shook her head. For years she had seen Jenna take Jack for granted, not seeing the handsome, patient, funny guy right under her nose who had supported her in whatever madcap idea she wanted to do. Ignoring the irony of her own situation with Marcus, she couldn't help but respond in a way that she knew would more than likely upset her. "But you haven't been together for nearly a year Jenna. Surely, you're not expecting him to stay glued to you. After all, you both agreed to have a break, didn't you?"

"Yes, we're on a "break," she said, emphasising "break", "but it was only whilst I got my business up and running. You know we've kept in touch and meet up regularly" she retorted, as a picture of him looking trendy and fit in the coffee shop the last time they met, flashed before her. She felt a pang of jealousy that came from the pit of her stomach as she recalled him mentioning his new boss was a woman.

"I'm sure it's nothing Jen," Carrie assured her. "Jack has always worked with women and adores you. You both decided for some space between you for a short while, that shouldn't mean a complete break-down of your relationship, should it?"

The truth was that Jenna didn't know if the short break had an end to it or if it was being deferred by the month. What she did know is that neither Jack nor she had discussed the reality of the situation, if there were any ground rules, and if so, where the repercussions might lead. "Oh God," she groaned, "what have I done?"

Carrie put the kettle on whilst searching for cups in various cupboards. Seizing the opportunity to speak to her without the others, Rachel busied herself helping, casually looking across to the others who were deep in conversation. "You haven't told me how it went with Marcus." Carrie's face remained non plussed whilst internally she squirmed with a combination of guilt and embarrassment. "What do you mean?" she asked casually.

"Did he say anything about me or the pregnancy?" Other than the fact that he's scared of the responsibility of having a ready-made family of four, the fact that his business is going under, and that he's not sure about how he feels about you, was what she really wanted to say. Carrie smiled resolutely and looked at Rachel. She knew this "thing" or whatever this was with Marcus had to stop.

"Rachel stop worrying, will you?" As far as I could tell, Marcus is just a bit stressed over work and needs a bit of support from you. I think you need to reconnect with him – why don't you go away somewhere before the babies are born?" Rachel nodded her head understanding, but the word 'reconnect' resonated and jumped out at her. Were her and Marcus so disconnected now that he preferred to talk to one of her friends rather than his wife, she pursed her lips wondering if Carrie had not given her the full unabridged version of events.

***

Carrie's face bent down as Marcus tasted the sweetness of her breath. The lingering kiss dissolved into a series of playful kisses on his neck and down to his chest. Her chestnut hair fell into silky folds across his torso as he put his hands through her hair stroking her gently. He groaned with desire and felt a wrench of love that came from his gut with a growing realisation that made his heart, beat faster. The dream was so real it woke him up with a surreal feeling of déjà vu. Disorientated, and clammy from sweat he lay quietly next to Rachel wondering what had just happened.

Jenna

Jenna was in trouble. She lay in the dark listening to the sound of rain pattering steadily on to the glass roof light above the antique bed that had been the marital bed for fifteen years. Fifteen years was a long time, in fact it was almost half her life, and now the possibility of not having Jack to continue to share it with consumed her with jealousy, as she revisited the scene where she saw him happy and laughing with another woman.

The idea that he was free to sleep with someone else hadn't entered her head when they agreed to have a break. She tried to recall the actual conversation they'd had when after many discussions and lamentations about her work, he had suggested that he gave her some space to grow her business. Was it a suggestion or was it mutual agreement? Was it his idea? She recalled the moment in her mind, knowing in the deep recess of her memory that it was his idea. Had that always been on the cards she wondered, did it just happen to be convenient for him to say it, like a get out of jail card that he'd been keeping under cover waiting for the right time to play his hand?

She reached across to her mobile and idly checked into Facebook with a nagging feeling of anxiety resonating in the pit of her stomach. Jack wasn't a user of Facebook, well at least whilst he was at home with her, he never used it. In fact, he most often moaned about social media and its dominance over her and the boys.

Casually she typed his name into the search bar. Twenty profiles popped up. She scrolled through, knowing that he had an account set up by one of the boys but did not use it, but curiosity overcame her as she found his profile and opened his page. His profile picture was new, showing a tanned, smiling face and longer hair style. Jenna felt cheated and violated although she was not sure why. She clicked through photos which seemed to feature a lot of football and sports photos of his team until her eye spotted the slim figure of a woman in jeans on the touchline.

She zoomed in to take a closer look realizing that it was the same woman he had walked out of the office with when she had hoped to take him to lunch. The candid shot skilfully captured her clapping and laughing as Jack was taking a corner. Jenna felt sick. She turned off the phone as her self-esteem took the biggest hit for months, plunging her further into despondency. Perhaps it was the shock, or genuine tiredness, but the sleep came suddenly as she closed her eyes and fell into a deep unconscious slumber.

***

The chink of light that peeped through the curtains directed itself on to Jenna's face waking her up. She squinted and rolled over to check the time. Nine thirty in the morning, she had slept soundly for ten hours. She could not remember the last time she had slept for so long and sat up abruptly trying to recall if it was a school day. Momentary panic over when the radio confirmed it was Saturday. She sat back against the pillow with a strange sense of calm as she took the notebook lying on her bedside table and began writing.

The affirmations came thick and fast, free flowing; a stream of consciousness that came from her core "I Jenna Clarkson am happily married with a husband who loves me for who I am." I Jenna Clarkson am a confident, fun-loving desirable woman. "I Jenna Clarkson have a loving husband who still loves me unconditionally." She filled the remaining pages, carefully put the book in a drawer, and stepped into the shower energised and ready for battle. There was no way that she was going to let a trivial photograph and momentary lapse in sensibility lose her husband and marriage.

Carrie

Ben pulled up outside Carrie's flat and beeped the horn. He had a good feeling about the weekend ahead and was in buoyant mood. The first wave of late summer heat had broken through the cotton wool cloud to unveil pure blue skies and a warmth that had begun to seep into the pavement. It reminded him of home – Cape Town home. The home that he had left ten years before to start a new life in Europe, and one that would help him start again. He idly texted Carrie "How are you getting on? I'm outside." Immediately the response "Soz, just sorting a few things out, I'll be there in 10. Come in?" In the few short months, he'd got to know Carrie, he knew that if he went in, ten minutes would become twenty, after the coffee and inevitable final work email check. "No, I'm fine, I'll stay here. I'm on a yellow line."

He sat back and turned the radio on. "Is it getting better, or do you feel the same? Will it make it easier on you now, you've got someone to blame?" The U2 lyrics resounded loudly and took him back to the party where he'd finally plucked up the courage to end it with Julie-Anne, his girlfriend of five years. In hindsight, the party was not the best place to do it but walking on the beach afterwards, alone together, he took the opportunity to tell her that he didn't love her anymore. Ben had never ended a relationship before as everything pre-Julie-Anne were just casual flings that seemed to have a natural timeline that petered out in a mutually convenient way.

"Did I disappoint you, leave a bad taste in your mouth? You act like you never had love and you want me to go without." He recalled the look of horror and hurt in her face as she crumpled and fell to the sand sobbing. Tough love his mum would call it, she never liked Julie-Anne anyway and for some reason their personalities clashed. He had let things go on for far too long and knew that the relationship had run its course two years before, but he'd let it go and ignored the demons in his head. Now two years later, he thought he'd turned a corner until he had heard from his best mate Thabo that she had accused him of rape. He knew she had a vindictive, reckless streak in her and had seen it once or twice over the years, confirming his feelings that she wasn't *the one*. He should have got out of the toxic relationship earlier but somehow the months had turned to years as he focused on his career and let his true feelings take a back seat.

He knew Thabo was innocent, there wasn't an aggressive bone in his body, and he had an inherent and natural kindness and respect towards all people including women. His best friend since childhood, Ben and Thabo had a shared history and respect which continued into their adult life. He had done everything he could to try and persuade her to withdraw her claim, but the hurt and humiliation he had put on to her had turned to anger, and there was no way that Julie-Anne was going to let this go. The guilt and responsibility lay heavy on his shoulders, but his hope was that the money he was giving to Thabo's sister to pay for the English lawyer would finally get his name cleared.

Meeting Carrie on New Year's Eve was serendipity. She was seemingly, the most beautiful, kind, fun loving woman he had ever come across, but he was definitely playing it safe this time round. No way was he going to plunge into something again unless, he was sure.

He glanced up as Carrie slid gracefully into the seat beside him and kissed him on the cheek smiling. "Sorry. You should know by now that people give me false deadlines! I always seem to have an endless list of things to do."

"I hope you've left your work phone at home so that we can relax properly," he said, turning to her as the car's engine revved. "I have as it happens." She said blushing, and not understanding why she found him so scarily cool. The fact that she could not read him was something to do with it she pondered, as they drove off heading for the Dorset coast. It was quite nice, they were good friends who enjoyed being together, the fact that he hadn't tried it on with her since the party was refreshing, but also left her feeling unsettled and unsure about how he felt about her. He smiled with genuine warmth in his eyes and squeezed her hand. A charge of electricity emanated from the simple, brief touch but spoke a myriad of unsaid words and feelings between them.

***

The hotel suite over-looked the meandering river and meadow at the top of the traditional, thatched manor house, but details of the view and surroundings were lost as soon as they closed the door behind them. Feeling Ben's hands gently guiding her face, Carrie fell into his kiss, accepting that her life was about to become even more complicated. They moved on to the bed and carried on enjoying the moment and new-found intimacy. Finally, he pulled away and propped himself up on his elbow and looked at Carrie intently with his clear green eyes. His fingers traced her lips as she shuddered wanting more from him. "Carrie, you know I really like you, don't you?"

"I really like you too," she murmured and pulled him towards her wondering if their friendship had taken a new level.

Chapter 11

September

Rachel

Marcus took another swig of beer and leant back on the sofa with his feet on the coffee table in front of him flicking the remote until he found the football match he had been looking forward to all day. Rachel was out and he at last had the house to himself, a rare occasion these days as she never seemed to leave the inner sanctum. Maybe he should get himself a shed he contemplated, then at least he'd have his own space, perhaps get a few mates round for a beer and a game of pool or watch the footie together. Chelsea were winning 2:1 against his childhood team Man United, he finished the beer and cracked open another bottle feeling a sense of freedom and relief that he could spend the afternoon idling away in front of the TV without Rachel nagging him in the background.

Had things really got that bad, he wondered, or was it just his imagination. It seemed that she was constantly on at him to do various chores and was ready to pounce if he either had not done them because he hadn't got around to it or didn't like the way he'd done them. I mean, why is it so important to scrape every last morsel off a plate before it goes in the bloody dishwasher, they're made to wash the bloody dishes aren't they? The house was littered with baby stuff everywhere and he was feeling increasingly stifled.

He looked at his phone and went to Facebook. As usual, plenty of arseholes pretending their lives were perfect and the regular stupid jokes and political statements. He hated Facebook but knew it was his only glimpse into Carrie's life even though she didn't use it that much, compared to the other girls in the group.

He opened her page as nothing was on his feed, even if she hadn't posted anything it gave him a chance to see her face and imagine that they were together. Her status had changed to "Rare weekend break in Dorset" with her hair blowing in the wind and laughing freely. God she was beautiful – he knew she wasn't with the girls so perhaps a work colleague he contemplated hopefully. He scrolled down the feed and saw Ben, the guy from the New Year's Eve party wearing Police shades staring to the camera with the sea in the background. A rage of jealousy hit him in the chest knowing that they were together. How dare she go with him, she was his, they had a secret arrangement, an agreement in fact.

Three beers into the afternoon and Marcus had lost sight of any rationality and wanted to pick up the phone and call Carrie immediately, furious that she was not exclusive to him alone, they had a special relationship and were best mates for fuck's sake! He pressed auto dial and waited for the number to connect. It rang three times before he came to his senses and hung up. Carrie on the other hand was too preoccupied to care as she lay in the arms of Ben, naked and between the sheets.

***

Rachel was exhausted. She waddled into the house a day earlier than planned. The weekend trip with her mum had come to an abrupt halt when her mum had a migraine that morning and she knew that she would be out for the count for the rest of the day, lying in a darkened room. The baby shopping spree had been planned for weeks and Rachel had been looking forward to spending the day and night in Brighton indulging herself before the birth of the twins in a month's time.

The evening before, she'd had a lovely time with 'Mummy and Daddy', still sticking to the childhood term and similarly, enjoying the attention they lavished on their little girl. The subject of Marcus had inevitably come round once again during the meal, and Rachel had hoped that she had managed to deflect most of their innuendos, but to be honest she reflected, she could not help but agree with some of their thinking, deciding it best to keep her thoughts to herself. Was he lazy? She couldn't decide.

He worked long hours every day providing her with the life she aspired to, but did he do anything above and beyond? He did want to have a family; well, he did eighteen months before, when they were still trying through IVF. Now though, she wasn't so sure, but why would he change in such a short space of time, they had been trying and talking about it for six years previously. In fact, was it eighteen months before when things seemed to change or was it longer? She recalled the first year they tried for IVF, there was so much hope between them followed by so much disappointment.

They kept going though; the frequent clinic visits, the check-ups, the thermometer to check her temperature, and so it went on but somehow after that first attempt, his spark went, and it was never quite the same.

She pushed open the door and squeezed herself through the gap laden with bags and overnight suitcase. "Hello darling." She called out peeping into the lounge. The deep sleep that Marcus was in failed to wake him up, the beer bottles, debris, and TV, clearly showing how he had spent the afternoon. Rachel set about clearing up, making no effort to hide the ensuing noise. He woke with a jerk disorientated. "What the fu.." "Hello to you too!" Rachel said huffily as she picked up the bottles around her.

"What day is it?" Marcus said not sure if he had slept through the entire weekend. "It's Saturday evening for God's sake! What day do you think it is?" Rachel replied tight lipped. "I thought you weren't back 'til Sunday?" he said blinking and sitting up.

"Yes, I can see that!" she responded without looking at him as she cleared the remaining clutter. "Give me a break will you," said Marcus, finding himself annoyed and aggrieved that she had invaded his weekend. "What's happened?" he asked not really interested in the answer.

"Mum woke up with a migraine is what happened and so I've come home. You know she's completely zonked when she has an attack."

"Oh, sorry to hear that," Marcus said standing up and stretching. "The thing is hon, I'd made plans, you know, going out with the boys and all that." He said, lying and not looking her in the eye.

"That's fine. You do whatever you want. I can't do much these days, the size I am," Rachel said, holding back the tears.

"Ok if you're really sure. I can always stay at home with you," he replied unconvincingly. The truth was that Marcus had given himself a get out of jail card but didn't know how to use it. He knew that his mates were away at a football match that weekend because he'd been invited but was so broke, he turned it down and used the excuse of work to opt out. Was there a movie he could go to perhaps? Drinking on your own in the pub was a bit sad, he couldn't do that.

He turned to Rachel and kissed her lightly on the cheek, "I'll be back later tonight as long as you'll be OK. Call me on the mobile if you need me." He walked out reaching for his car keys and texted Carrie, "Are you around by chance? Could really do with a mate right now, no strings."

Rachel

I catch a glimpse into Marcus's life without me. A fly on the wall. An observer if only for a few minutes but one that sees the truth thrown back in my face. My usually pristine home is a trail of devastation and chaos, with beer bottles and takeaway cartons leaving little room on the coffee table. My sleeping, dishevelled husband is oblivious to the sound of the television playing sport as well as my entrance and absence. I am at first dismayed, then angry. The anger rises in me and protects the hurt that I feel inside. Yet another example that he doesn't care.

I begin to clear the mess and deliberately make a noise. I want him to wake up and to be disturbed from his cosy other life, one that does not appear to include me. I deliberately crash around and brush against his head leaning on the arm of the sofa as I walk past. He opens his eyes and first looks at me suspiciously upside down. I don't like to feel that I'm an intruder in my own home, that I need permission to return, and when I do return, my home doesn't feel like mine. It feels like a bachelor pad, not the family home I have spent years creating.

I want Marcus to go out. I want to return to normality and shield myself from this other persona who I do not know. Where is the Marcus who I was in love with? I use the past tense as I speak to myself and hear the words that for the first time make me question if I feel the same now as I did then.

Chapter 12

Hattie

Hattie woke up dazed and looked across at the peaceful figure of Francoise lying next to her. Did last night really happen? She knew she had drunk a lot but was also fully aware of what she was doing. She propped herself up on her elbow and followed the curve of her side and slim back, her long, elegant neck and short spikey hair dishevelled from sleep, proper bedhead, she thought smiling. "Stop it," mumbled Francoise sleepily. "Stop what?" Hattie whispered into her ear. "Stop staring at me. I can feel your eyes penetrating my back," she said good humouredly.

"Well, turn around then."

Francoise turned to face her, squinting with one eye as a chink of light from the half-open curtain fell upon her face. "In France we always prefer to kiss rather than make conversation," she said smiling. Words were substituted by kisses, sentences were formed by touch, feelings overtook conversation with a complicit understanding between them that required no further explanation.

Two hours later over brunch in the local pub, Francoise's hand gently brushed against Hattie's arm as she leaned across to pass some condiments. The electric current made the soft blonde hair on her forearm stand up in response. "Hey steady, I don't know why, but I feel quite giddy," Hattie said with flushed cheeks. "Probably too much partying."

"I don't think we'd ever have too much partying Hattie." She replied quietly.

"You unnerve me Francoise, I don't know why but you do. I don't know what happened last night, but I have a family and a husband."

"And..?"

"Well, I need to get back and do what I have to do!

I'm a mother remember, I can't just swan off and bat for the other side, for want of a better phrase." She gulped and looked down into the half-drunk cappuccino.

"But you already have Hattie."

"No! You know how much I think of you Francoise, but I'm mixed up, fucked up in fact. I don't know what I want or who I am."

"I know who you are Hattie. You're a free spirit that has been kept locked up for far too long. It's time to let go, to rediscover your creativity, to unleash your inhibitions, and enjoy what you want to do. I know you have a family, but does that really matter? We can still be friends and have time together surely?"

Hattie looked up glassy eyed, "I'm scared."

"No need to be my darling. I'll hold your hand all the way." She said, reaching across the table. Their fingers touched and entwined briefly until Hattie pulled away.

***

Hattie parked the car quietly outside the house, a cloud of guilt hovered over her exacerbated by the lateness of the hour, which meant that she had missed the children's bedtime. Trying to be absolve her guilt and fear, she pushed the weekend to the back of her mind so that the detail of who she saw, what she did, and how she felt, was put into a box of "I'll deal with that later" as she turned the key with a heavy heart expecting aggravation from Rob.

All was quiet when she entered the spotless kitchen whose tiles shone brightly, and kitchen work tops gleamed. Gone was the grubby grout and fingerprinted cupboards, the wooden floor had been polished and the whole place smelled of fresh linen. Pausing, she pushed the lounge door open to see Rob's laptop placed on the shelf of the coffee table, papers cleared away and even cushions had been plumped, perhaps she should go away more often she thought. Carrying on with a tour of the house she climbed the stairs and opened the girls' bedroom. Sprawled on the bed, lay Rob, asleep with both girls on either side with his arms round them, their story book lay open on his chest.

Hattie's heart melted seeing her family and wondered why she couldn't do this. How come when she's on her own because of Rob's work, the house is chaotic, and the girls' rooms are a jumble of clothes, toys, and general clutter, which trickles all the way down the stairs, infiltrating every room in the house. One night away and he has cleaned the entire house, made the dinner, put the washing on and got the girls to sleep. Clearly knackered though she thought looking at her husband fast asleep. She crept downstairs to pour herself a glass of wine as the familiar ping of a text came through. "How is everything? I can't stop thinking about you. The weekend was amazing." She pinged a heart emoji back with two kisses "me too but better go as kids need me." She hoped they did but was wracked with fear that perhaps they did not need her as much as she thought after all.

Jenna

"*Hi, I am Radhika Mehta and I am getting married this week. I am twenty-seven years old. I grew up in Delhi. I now work in London, at Goldman Sachs an investment bank. I am vice president in the Distressed Debt Group. Thank you for reading my story. However, let me warn you. You may not like me too much. One, I make a lot of money. Two, I have an opinion on everything. Three I've had sex. Now if I was a guy you would be okay with all of this. But since I am a girl these things don't really make me too likeable do they?*"
("One Indian Girl" – Chetan Bhagat)

Jenna turned the page absorbed in the story as she lay against the pillow sipping tea before she finally closed her eyes. This was too close for comfort she thought feeling a sense of déjà vu into her old life working in the corporate world of city finance. She thought back to the days of the daily commute into London's financial district and hardly recognised who she was back then. Could she really have led a team of hedge fund managers? But she did of course, although it felt as if she was looking back at somebody who was completely different to the person she had become. She remembered the sharp suits she wore, the killer heels and tailored shirts. She did look good admittedly, as she recalled the inevitable flirting that took place on most days. She

142

thrived in the male dominated environment, enjoying the respect she had gained, as well as the laughs and banter that went between them all. How on earth did she do it she questioned, as she glanced across to the mirror to see two-year old PJs, and her loose faded T-shirt, that should have been thrown out long ago.

She was good at her job, she knew that, but somehow, she had lost her way after the boys were born, finding it increasingly difficult and stressful juggling work, career, and motherhood, so something had to give. They had struggled with various au pairs and nannies over the years but just could not find a way to make it work. The long days, missing bedtime, and missing sports days, football matches and other parenting milestones began to take its toll as Jack began to suggest that she gave up work. Now on reflection, she wondered if the landscaping business idea was his way of appeasing her, merely seeing it as a hobby that she could do on the side. Jenna however, had other plans and saw this as an opportunity to get out of the rat race and put her energy into a new career and continue earning the income she was used to.

Handing in her resignation to her boss wasn't easy and the decision to leave had taken several months. "Don't do it Jenna. You're a great asset to us, have you thought this through?" He questioned when they went for a lunchtime drink and she broke the news. She had done nothing else but think things through over previous months but never reached a satisfactory solution. Jack's constant cajoling did not help.

It was a knee jerk reaction and perhaps she should not have been pushed into it after all, she thought, resentment building inside her. She had sunk most of her savings into the landscaping business and was now on the brink of bankruptcy, how did that happen? Being a single parent is what happened she thought bitterly. Left to look after the boys whilst Jack just doing the niceties of parenting, she had no time or energy to focus on the important details, such as financial forecasting, budgeting, and marketing.

Now as she continued to struggle on her own, he had managed to find the time to play football, lose weight, buy new clothes, and meet somebody else. Despite everything she missed him and ached to feel his arms around her once more.

***

The hairdresser spoke to the mirror bearing Jenna's reflection, "So it's a complete restyle then, is it?" "Absolutely," she responded without hesitation. "I want to go short, feathered layers, and get some ash blonde highlights put in." The hairdresser held a lock of the shoulder length bob and twisted it with his fingers. "Okay, let's get you washed, and we'll get going," he said smiling, as he gestured to a junior to take over for the hair wash.

At a hundred and fifty pounds a pop this was a serious investment in the new Jenna who was determined to reinvent herself and pull back some semblance of her old self. She closed her eyes and allowed the Indian head massage to mask the guilt she was beginning to feel.

The haircut was symbolic she told herself as more and more hair fell to the ground and a youthful reflection began to emerge in the facing mirror. Teasing out the style with mousse Jenna's favourite hairdresser looked across smiling "It's fab. Really suits you," he said beginning to blow dry it into feathery tendrils that framed her small face. "Why don't you get your make up done whilst you're here? We have a junior beautician who has just started and could do with some practice."

Jenna hesitated, trying to think of an excuse which was quickly counteracted when the young girl walked over and gestured to the beauty area. "It'll only take twenty minutes," she said encouragingly. Well, I can't imagine how much makeup she'll plaster me in for twenty minutes but in for a penny, she convinced herself, getting caught up in the momentum.

She followed the junior into the beauty area hidden from the rest of the salon for privacy. Not one for wearing make-up and nothing more than the occasional slick of lipstick, half an hour later she peered into the mirror not recognising the young, healthy glow of her skin, and bright eyes enhanced by subtle highlighter and natural blush. She wasn't sure, but did she actually look younger than when she had walked in two hours before. She paid for her treatment and bounced out of the salon trying to stop herself from smiling inanely.

Get a grip Jenna she muttered internally as she browsed the clothes aisle in the small, exclusive, boutique. The stress of the business and looking after the boys alone had contributed to the stone in weight, she had lost over the past six months. "Are you looking for anything in particular?" the young sales assistant asked duty bound. "No just browsing," came the stock response. She was left alone to consider the boyfriend jeans, loose T-shirt and leather flip flops she had somehow managed to convince herself to try in the changing room.

A hundred- and fifty-pounds lighter, she walked out of the shop wearing all three new purchases and called Jack on speed dial. "What are you up to today?" she asked casually.

"No plans really, why? Is something wrong?" he asked in his softly spoken northern accent. "Jack, I don't just contact you when something is wrong," Jenna said huffily, trying to curb her tendency to be defensive all the time. He stopped himself from disagreeing, tired of the usual verbal ping pong. "OK, so what's up?"

"Well, I'm not far from you at the moment, I've just been to the hairdresser and well, wondered if you fancied lunch?" He hesitated and considered his options but almost instantly agreed, well what the hell, they hadn't seen each other for over a month, and it would be good to see her.

The Hut was a casual restaurant and bar decorated with Hawaiian themed masks, wooden artefacts and planting that screened the tables and seating giving privacy to diners. Outside there was a covered wooden deck and additional dining areas overlooking a landscaped garden with a water feature. Rob walked into the restaurant and adjusted his eyes to the low light looking for Jenna. Not overly crowded, it should have been possible to find somebody without too much trouble but no sign of her. He walked through the bar and on to the deck and then heard her voice calling to him. His eyes followed the soft tone and rested on the slim blonde woman in the corner with the slow realisation that it was Jenna, transformed, stunning, and completely different.

"Ta dah!" she smiled standing up to embrace him. "What do you think?" she said with a mischievous grin. "I think you look amazing," he said, sitting next to her. "You've bought new clothes as well, they suit you. Different to your usual style," he said approvingly as he picked up the menu.

Jenna was in the mood for fun. This was the first weekend in months where both the boys were away at friends' houses and not back until Sunday. No taxi service to football and then on to their mates, no supermarket shop, and no washing their clothes ready for various parties. She sat back and looked at her husband wondering if the fire in their relationship could be ignited once more. "Let's have a bottle of wine," she suggested. One bottle became two and food followed, after long conversations about everything and anything, except themselves and what they had been doing, or how they felt about things. It was as if the past year hadn't happened and they were just out for the day enjoying each other's company. Jack was on form, and his dry sense of humour that had attracted Jenna in the first place, continued to entertain her.

It was five o'clock when they stumbled out, happily drunk in the taxi together that was to take them back to the house - their home, their family's anchor. Rob still had a key and turned the lock making Jenna's heart burst with happiness. They closed the door and fumbled their way upstairs to the bedroom, pulling off clothes from each other, kissing, caressing, biting. It was the best sex Jenna could remember having. Jack was toned and fit, the familiarity of knowing each other's body, their likes, dislikes, and how they fitted together made it easy, comforting, and sensual. But the bubble of hope burst and showered Jenna with despair and insecurity when hours later Jack turned, leaning towards her, and said, "Jen, there's something I have to tell you. I've met somebody else."

Carrie

Carrie returned to work energised and excited. She hadn't been in a relationship for over a year and was beginning to enjoy the intimacy of a close relationship that had seemingly moved to a new level from friendship to boyfriend. Déjà vu she wondered, thinking about Marcus but quickly acknowledged that they were not in a "relationship" and as far as she was concerned it wasn't going to happen again anyway. It was time to move on and put this episode in their lives behind them.

However, the Thabo friendship troubled her and even though Ben had explained that he didn't know she was the lawyer working on the case, a seed of doubt had been planted, but she also knew in her heart that if she was to continue on the case, she would not be able to see him because of the conflict of interest.

***

Julie-Anne put down the phone and gulped the last drop of prosecco in her glass. She looked out on to the swimming pool in the landscaped gardens of her family's house as a wave of shame swept across her.

She hadn't intended for things to go this far but she was in so deep she had no idea how she could get out of it. The iMessage from her friend with a photo of the article in the paper saying that Thabo Mwansa was in hospital after being beaten up by other in-mates filled her with horror. She replied with an emoji face crying and turned her phone off.

The belligerent act of revenge on her ex started purely as a knee jerk reaction to Ben's news that he did not love her – he didn't even say "anymore" as if he'd never loved her at all. She was bereft and hurt and needed him to suffer as much as her. Julie-Anne's opinion of Thabo was that he controlled Ben, the longstanding "bromance" between the two of them dominated him so that he would always defend his friend if she ever raised the subject. She knew that Thabo had never liked her and had always thought of her as shallow, how dare he she thought, as a rising anger made its way up through her body.

Get a grip Julie-Anne she told herself as she poured another drink thinking things through. It wasn't pre-meditated she tried to convince herself, after all surely, in all those police dramas on TV, it's the pre-meditated, planned attacks that get jail surely? All she'd done was to make a claim that a well-respected doctor had tried it on with her, well that was the plan, but somehow when she told the nurse on duty in the ward, it became a much bigger thing than she had intended. In fact, there was so much fuss, and so many people involved, interviewing her, and writing notes, that she had no choice but to make it a bit more dramatic. They put words in my mouth she thought trying to deflect the blame.

I'm sure I didn't actually say it was rape, attack perhaps, but not rape, and I also said that I'd changed my mind about registering the claim. But by the time they had typed the report as she recounted the event, there was no way that she could take it away.

The rising panic in her body showed itself in red blotches on her neck and cheeks which usually occurred when she was stressed. Her mother who lay on the sun lounger nearby looked across concerned. "Baby, are you OK? You're looking a bit flushed darling, perhaps you've had too much sun?" she called across in her softly spoken Afrikaans accent. "I'm fine mum," Julie-Anne responded feebly, holding back the tears she pulled her baseball cap over her eyes and lay back down.

***

The weekly visit to her therapist usually took Julie-Anne along the residential suburban streets of Cape Town's middle-class elite. Large, gated, houses with perfectly manicured lawns and palm trees emanated a picture of domesticity and money. Sprinklers spun their web of water across carpets of green, whilst domestic staff busied themselves with their various chores.

This was the life Julie-Anne had grown up with, never questioning the inequality between her family and the staff who worked for them, until she met Thabo Mwansa.

150

Up until then, she had never met or knew anybody from a black township, let alone socialised with them. Ben's introduction to his best friend at a bar when they had just met was so unexpected that she didn't know how to react. She remembered feeling flushed and wasn't sure what to say in rare moment of embarrassment.

Her stiff, controlled smile failed to put him off though as Thabo's cheeky, twinkling eyes continued to laugh with Ben over mutual jokes that could only have been understood after years of friendship and unconditional love and respect for each other. And so, from the very first meeting, the seed of jealousy was sown, continuing to grow over the years as she struggled to come to terms with a friendship that appeared to be stronger than her own relationship.

"So how have you been?" the flamboyantly dressed psychotherapist asked. The fifty something Doctor of Psychology and personal therapist sat back in the leather armchair and crossed her legs waiting for response. "Not good" she responded looking down at her hands. The therapist waited, notebook in hand using her experience to allow the silence.

"We broke up," Julie Anne eventually explained. She continued, "Ben told me that he didn't love me. I don't know why. We were so good together for five years," she said as the tears started to fall.

"Why do you think he decided to tell you after all this time? Has something happened?"

The anger resurfaced as Julie-Anne looked up "Nothing has happened. My guess is that his stupid best mate has finally persuaded him to leave me" she said shrugging her shoulders and wiping her eyes.

"Tell me about Ben's best friend. Why don't you like him?" the line of gentle questioning persisted. "I never said I didn't like him." Silence. Realising that the Therapist wasn't going to fill the gap, she continued reluctantly. "I don't want to talk about him, why do I have to talk about him?" she asked irritated that Thabo had once again infiltrated her personal space.

"Julie-Anne you seem to have anger issues around this friendship. If you are to move on with your development, it is important that you can let go of this. Stay with me on this please. So just talk to me about it, what's his name?"

"I'd rather not say," Julie-Anne responded with an air of petulance. "OK, then why are you convinced that your break-up is to do with this person?"
"Can I talk about me instead please?"
"OK, what do you want to talk about?" the Therapist said looking up above her glasses, eyebrows raised.
"I've done something that I shouldn't have, and everything has gone wrong, and I can't change things." Julie Anne whispered leaning forward, as she put her elbows on her knees and head in her hands.
"Want to tell me about it?" the Therapist said gently prompting.

The burden of the lie rested heavily on Julie-Anne's shoulders as she realised that she had a choice lying right in front of her. A decision so important that it would shape her future and the future of several other people. A tear drop trickled down her cheek as the Therapist leaned forward and passed a tissue across.

The prolonged two-hour session left Julie Anne feeling exhausted as she pulled away from the drive and headed towards the police station. She knew that the situation she had caused had gone on long enough and whilst her moral compass had strayed violently the wrong way and towards selfishness and self-pity, she also knew that she had to change things if she was to be able to live with herself in the future.

The mix of relief and anxiety overwhelmed her as she parked in a layby to phone home.

Rachel

Marcus was still out as Rachel lay in bed uncomfortably hot. Her stomach was hard as the skin across her abdomen stretched taut with no room to give. She propped herself up on an elbow and gently lay down on her side with a pillow between her legs. Gone were the blooming cheeks and sexy look of the just rounded tum and growing round breasts. Now in the final trimester, Rachel felt like a beached whale and hated her body, covering it up with a loose, over-sized long t-shirt and the constant maternity bra that had become her go to wardrobe basic for the past few months. She felt sick, and slowly raised herself up again and leaned against the headboard with a pillow propped up behind her.

She didn't feel right and tried lying down again easing herself down slowly on to her back rubbing her stomach.

There it was again. Her stomach felt as if somebody had taken the smallest remaining skin that could be pinched and pulled it again, taut. The pain lasted a minute and then left her body, but she still felt sick. She looked at the clock on the bedside table – 1am.

By the time Marcus had got the five texts, two voicemails and two missed calls, Rachel was seven centimetres dilated and sitting on the edge of the hospital bed in the private room that her parents had paid for. He cautiously walked into the room, breathless from running down the corridor. "I'm sorry darling, I shouldn't have left you. The pub had a lock in, and you know there's no signal there. Are you OK?" he said rubbing her back.

"Shut up Marcus. You're here now" Rachel responded preoccupied with the increasing pain she was experiencing. A mid-wife opened the door smiling and looked over to Marcus. "Oh good, Dad is here finally. How are you doing my dear?" She said walking over to Rachel whilst checking the monitor propped up near the bed.

"I feel sick," said Rachel in tears. The overwhelming pain took over her body again making her even more nauseous. She vomited into the disposable cardboard container the midwife held under her chin. "It's perfectly normal dear. Sometimes the contractions can make some women sick. Now let me check you again." The midwife gently helped Rachel on to the bed and prised her legs open to see how things were progressing. "Bit of pain for a bit darling. Big breath," she encouraged, as she looked to see the beginning of a new life that was due to enter the world.

"OK, we are ready. You're fully dilated and so just go with me. When I say push, you take a big breath and push through OK."

Rachel's forehead was wet with perspiration. With flushed cheeks she held on to Marcus's hand and looked at him imploringly. "Don't leave me Marcus, will you?" The question shook him to the core as he interpreted it with double innuendo. "Of course, I won't darling, I'm here for you," he said, squeezing her hand.

If he had a choice, Marcus would run away. Run away as far as possible, to somewhere where no-one could find him, and he could start again. He'd have no responsibilities, no stress from his business and he could be the person he wanted to be. He would run a beach bar, go surfing, and just chill in the mid-day sun. He looked at his wife's blotched face and damp hair and smiled encouragingly holding his fear back. Here they were bringing two new lives into the world together as the enormity of the situation came to the forefront of his consciousness. What the fuck had he been doing all this time with Carrie he wondered. He knew it was wrong and he hated what he had become but he just could not help himself.

Rachel screamed as a contraction reached its peak and the midwife continued to encourage her to follow her direction with her breathing. He felt helpless and a bit of a spare part, an on-looker even, somewhat removed from the situation.

Why was it that even in such a life-changing moment, that Carrie continued to dominate his thoughts? How would he feel if it was her lying there and not Rachel? Were these feelings about Rachel or about becoming a father and relinquishing the life he had known for the last twenty years? He was scared. Scared for the future, scared for his independence, and scared for Rachel, and the potential decision he could make that could affect both their lives.

Later, an all-consuming love enveloped Marcus as he held the tiny bodies in his arms. He was not sure where it had come from or how, but somehow the vulnerability of the tiny lives he held took over feelings of claustrophobia. Little did he know, the fear would return, and he would have to face it again later.

Chapter 13

October

Hattie

"She was sitting behind a desk in the smallest office on the highest floor of the UNICEF building. Her appearance confirmed my worst fears: she was beautiful" ("Impossible Journey" – Michael Asher)

The group of friends sat on the floor of Rachel's lounge as she breast-fed the two boys, one on each breast. It was an odd sight which seemed to change the dynamic of the group from a night out to put the world to rights over a bottle or two of wine, to a creche and an endless stream of baby anecdotes. Hattie and Jenna now firmly passed the baby stage had long stopped talking about the wonderous joys and woes of parenting and Carrie was so far removed from that lifestyle that she believed she had no right or inclination to give advice or sympathy.

They made a feeble attempt to discuss the book around the chaos that surrounded them. "Do you ever look at other women and see their attractiveness?" Hattie asked casually to no-one in particular. "All the time darling, all the time," said Jenna. "I'm always looking at other women and wondering why I can't be like them."

"Yes, but that's just reacting to the pressure put upon women to look good by media, isn't it? I meant, do you ever find other women, attractive in the male sense?" Hattie tried again.

"What? Do you mean in a sexual way?" Jenna responded, suddenly interested as all idle chit chat stopped to take in the answer. "I don't know, I suppose so," Hattie said limply. "Why do you ask? Do you?" Carrie interjected. "Oh God, I don't know Cass, no I'm not like that, well I don't think I am anyway," she said shrugging her shoulders smiling.

The babies began crying breaking the silence of the inner sanctum where secrets were divulged and remained unshared with anyone beyond the group. Rachel oblivious to the conversation gathered up the tiny bundles hushing and soothing as she removed herself upstairs to get them to sleep. Outwardly she seemed composed and in control, but reality was that she hadn't slept properly in a month, she had stopped eating, and could barely summon the energy to get up each day.

"Why do I get the feeling we were just about to get into a very interesting conversation" Jenna murmured under her breath as she caught Carrie's eye and winked.
"What have you been doing with yourself these days" Carrie asked, "You don't seem to be around much?". She said to Hattie.

"Not a lot really. I've been down to Cambridge for a few weekends now and again, that's all". "Ah visiting your new bestie," Jenna teased. "What's she like? Does Rob like her?"

"Rob hasn't met her actually, and yes she is nice, really nice in fact." There was no way Hattie was going to divulge anything else even to her closest friends, not yet anyway. She didn't even know how she felt about things herself, only that there was a yearning deep inside to keep seeing her, keep touching her, keep wanting her. Whether the growing desire was merely because of the novelty, or if it was the planting of a seed that was beginning to grow, she had no head space to consider what she thought, and how she felt. All she knew was that her weekend jaunts to Cambridge lifted her spirits and she became old Hattie, the person she always had been, rather than the Hattie who she had outwardly grown into.

"Tell us then. What's this new friend like?" Jenna asked again. "What does she look like?"

"She's French and lectures in art history at Cambridge."

"Why do you go there so often, doesn't Rob mind?" Jenna continued. "Bloody hell, what is this, the Spanish inquisition?" Hattie retorted somewhat heatedly.

Hattie's cheeks flushed as a feeling of heat made its way down her neck swathing her in perspiration. The room felt airless and claustrophobic, its chaotic contents strewn across the floor showing baby Armageddon, an amazing feat for two small boys who couldn't even sit up unaided.

Rachel walked into the room with a muslin cloth on her shoulder, hair dishevelled. She threw herself on to the bespoke designer armchair "freedom!" she sighed closing her eyes, oblivious to the chaos around her and the conversation that had begun between her friends. Hattie walked out and put the kettle on in the kitchen leaving the door ajar. Jenna crept out and followed her. "Are you OK?" she asked putting a hand lightly on Hattie's shoulder. She continued as she searched cupboards for coffee cups. "I'm sorry if I pressed you about, is it Fabian, sorry I can't remember her name?"

"It's Francoise actually. And don't worry about it Jen, she's staying at mine this weekend as Rob's away and so why don't we go out and have dinner together? Cass might want to join as well?" The response felt heavy in Hattie's throat, knowing that she was at the beginning of an emotional journey not knowing that later she was about to venture down a path she had never been down which had no end or defined beginning. They gathered up the cups and walked back into the lounge, whilst Jenna resisted the inclination to ask more questions.

"So, it's a girls' night out on Saturday then is it?" Jenna said lightly looking at Carrie. Hattie intervened explaining, "I said Francoise is staying at mine for the weekend as Rob's away. We're probably going to take the girls to the Tate and then Kensington Gardens or something like that, I've managed to get a babysitter so yeh, come out Sat evening," she said looking around. "Sorry amigos no can do," said Rachel shrugging. "Well, I'm in," Carrie said knowing that she would be at a loose end on Saturday without Ben.

***

The Jazz Café in Camden Lock continued to show off its eclectic charm as jazz funk sounds played amidst a sea of different ages and trendsetters. The dark ambiance of the upstairs gallery hid the slightly seedy nicotine-stained walls from years before but now covered with stylish black and white photos of musicians who had performed there over the years. The mezzanine and restaurant overlooked the dance floor, its tables occupied by couples and groups reflecting the diversity of London's inner city.

Carrie and Jenna made their way over to the table overlooking the stage where Hattie and Francoise were already tanked up from a previous bottle of prosecco. Huddled together Hattie was throwing her head back laughing, slightly turned towards her friend, who had her arm casually on the back of Hattie's chair. The pounding music and resounding chatter in the club bounced off the walls so that individuals were forced to compete by shouting to make themselves heard. Carrie and Jenna hadn't been to a "proper" club with music for so long that they felt out of touch but as eyes and ears adjusted, both knew that it was the perfect venue for the new Hattie who had emerged from the flames like a phoenix reborn.

They looked around and saw her, flame red hair and a mass of curls cascading down past her shoulders. An off the shoulder Bardot top was set off with tight dark pink cigarillo trousers and heels. As Hattie's weight continued to drop off, her bone structure emphasised the angle of her jaw and cheeks, whilst her collar bone was elegant and set off by strong, athletic shoulders and muscle toned arms.

Both friends had almost forgotten how attractive Hattie was and observed her from afar in a new light. Perhaps they had known her for so long they had forgotten who she was before children and marriage but there was no mistaking the old Hattie now. "Wait," said Carrie to Jenna as she was about to walk over. "Is that Hattie's new Cambridge friend? She's pretty stunning, isn't she?" They stopped briefly and observed the elegant confidence that seemed to ooze from Francoise who sat with poise and ease in a tight black silk jumpsuit and biker boots. Her short, feathered hair framed a face of delicate feline features and wide mouth. Dark red lipstick, her signature look gave an air of confidence and style whilst jewellery was minimal, apart from the four diamond earrings in her right ear including one at the top and two on the left.

The two friends exchanged looks and made their way over to the table almost feeling as if they were intruding. "Do you know what Cass," said Jenna holding a glass of wine in her hand, "If I didn't know better, I'd say they look like a couple."

Chapter 14

<u>Jenna</u>

Jenna's mood had been low for several weeks after Jack's confession that someone else was in his life. The momentary lapse of self-discipline fuelled by wine and afternoon sun had seeped into both their brains, allowing the hours that followed to become a passionate and exciting romp between the sheets.

For Jack it was also an opportunity to show Jenna how much he cared for her, but things had begun to change over the past few months as slowly he had found a new side to himself, one that enjoyed playing football, having fun and a beer with his mates, and of course the unequalled attention he got from his new colleague and boss. No longer was he competing with his kids for attention and being second in line for everything, in a world where the children always came first. He knew that the situation would revert as they got older but heck, he was forty already and did not want to waste his life waiting for something that might never happen.

Amanda, his colleague was a strong independent woman and without children. She had no ties and plenty of time and money to be decadent, and even hedonistic, such that they could spend all of Sunday in bed reading the papers, having sex and then going out for a late supper followed by indulgent box sets in bed and more sex. Had he ever done that with Jen, he couldn't recall. The fact that he had never questioned why Amanda didn't have children be it through choice or circumstance never crossed his mind, as he found himself falling in love again, whether this was with his new life, or a new person, he wasn't sure.

"Can you believe he had the gall to sleep with me and then tell me that he was seeing somebody else?" she said disparagingly to Rachel as they sat at their favourite table in the local coffee shop. The babies slept peacefully in their pram as Rachel yawned and touched her friend in sympathy unaware of the irony in her words. "Jen, why don't you just give him some space for a bit? You might find that this is just a bit of a release from the humdrum of family life. You said that it was the most passionate afternoon you'd ever had with him. That's got to stand for something hasn't it? He wouldn't have done it if he didn't have feelings for you or had stopped fancying you."

"I know but it's hard, I'm jealous and I'm scared. What if I've blown it and he decides that he wants to stay with her? I can't bear the thought of him being with someone else, enjoying himself and being intimate with somebody other than me."

"I know," Rachel said quietly, looking into her coffee. The two small words had a double innuendo that made Jenna look up with concern.

"Is everything Ok at home with you?"

"Not really," Rachel responded with a weak smile. "It wouldn't surprise me if Marcus was seeing somebody. We've become more and more distant ever since I first became pregnant. I know he's got a lot on his plate with his business and we do make love. But he's preoccupied all the time, he goes out a lot and he's mumbling things in his dreams. I only hear him as I'm awake to feed the boys three times a night."

"What do you mean, "mumbling things," Jenna said suddenly interested.

"I have no idea really Just funny stuff that makes no sense, something about Cass."

"Well, isn't his new development called Casper Street? It's bound to be about that. Don't worry about it." Jenna reassured.

"Yeh you're right I reckon. I'm just being overly sensitive. I've still got my baby fat, feel frumpy, and do need to get back into shape and stop being a yummy mummy I guess." She said shrugging, although inside a nagging doubt still lingered.

Carrie

The south African blue sky and sun led Carrie and Linda Mwansa to a cool spot under an umbrella in Cape Town's artisan sector. The crowded restaurant was full of office workers and friends meeting for lunch as they made their way to a table in the corner of the outdoor terrace away from the hub bub of noise.

They were talking about the deal Carrie was going to strike with Julie-Anne out of court since her confession to the police. The story hadn't yet broken with the newspapers, but it would only be a matter of time, and timing was crucial if Carrie was to secure the best financial and political outcome for her client.

She resisted asking about Ben although inwardly she was desperate to know his involvement and if he had said anything to Linda. "I told you my brother was innocent," Linda said, turning to Carrie. "And I always thought he was too. I'm so sorry that he was the victim of somebody else's revenge, but I will fight for the best deal I can get out of court, and I think we could be looking at around 500,000 rand as a minimum."

"Thabo won't take the money, I'm sure. He is only interested in getting his name cleared and getting back to his life."

"Nevertheless, there have been costs incurred for this case even though most of my work is pro-bono I know that there are still further expenses ensuing Linda. And if he doesn't want to take the money, use it to do something good with it, give it to a charity or even start a charitable project or whatever.

It's important that she doesn't get away with this, and an apology simply isn't enough. Carrie found herself responding heatedly. The dichotomous relationship between her professional and social life sat uneasily as Carrie over-compensated for her behaviour and guilt at home, determined to prove to herself that she was not a bad person.

Chapter 15

November

Rachel

I wish I am wearing jeans and a nice jacket as I look around the shop at the other new mums and then at my shapeless track suit bottoms. I feel self-conscious and touch my lank hair and try to comb it with my fingers. My reflection stares back at me in the baby mirror that I hold. I see a gaunt face which I barely recognise. My dull eyes show no emotion, I am not happy, I am not unhappy, I am existing.

My beautiful boys are asleep deep in their own world, protected in their pram. They are my secret, we have a secret, just the three of us, I like that. They deserve a present because they are so good. I look around at the couples wandering about and casually lift the blanket and put their presents underneath. A soft blue rabbit with floppy ears, a brown beanie dog with white patches.

I love the blue baby grows hanging on the rail, a pair of complementary colours, turquoise, and light blue. They would look so cute – I put them in the pram along with feeder cups, bottles, and anything else I think we need. It doesn't cross my mind to pay for anything. It's another secret, mine and the boys.

I finish my shopping and look around for Marcus and notice a small woman with wiry black hair looking at me from the other side of the store in the pram section.

Perhaps she has seen the baby grows and is thinking of getting the same. I smile at her and wend my way through the aisles towards the door. She seems to be following me, I notice puzzled, as anxiety begins to creep through my body.

I haven't done anything wrong, but people are beginning to stare because she's raising her voice and trying to get my attention "Excuse me! Excuse me madam." Madam? Is she calling me I wonder; my name isn't madam? I carry on towards the door but a tall man in his dark blue uniform crosses my path.

I am scared but I don't know why. I haven't done anything wrong. I want Marcus, but again he is not here; I am helpless as the small wiry haired woman is talking at me, saying things I don't understand. My babies are crying now – where is Marcus? Oh, here he is, late as usual and oblivious to the pain I am suffering.

***

The cool breeze and auburn haze of leaves gently drifting down to the pavement was a sure sign of the change of season and that autumn had taken its hold. Marcus turned up the collar of his jacket, idly leafing through his phone as he waited patiently for Rachel outside Mothercare. He leaned against the wall near the door absorbed in reading The Guardian sports page, oblivious to the shoppers around him. He hated these shopping trips, but if Rachel was happy, then he was happy, and there didn't seem to be many happy days recently.

"Hello mate!" He looked up to see his mate Freddo smiling broadly. "Doing the family duty? How are you doing? Haven't seen you at football much recently." Much to Marcus's frustration, football had been side lined these past few months as the chaos in the house seemed to indicate that Rachel wasn't coping.

Bins were left over-flowing, plates remained unwashed by the sink, and there was always a growing pile of clothes that never seemed to get from the laundry bin to the washing machine. The evenings after work were spent tidying up, getting a ready meal on, and making sure that the washing was done.

He had become a househusband but hadn't given up work. Was this what it would be like if he were a single parent he wondered. Chances are he contemplated, it might be easier or even better, at least he would have some control over his life rather than having a third child to look after, only this one is thirty-five years not two months old. "Hi Freddo, how are you? Yeh, I'm good thanks. You know what it's like with babies, they seem to take over your life!" he laughed falsely. "I know mate, just hold on to the fact it's only for a few years!" he grinned. "For fuck's sake, you're a bundle of joy, aren't you?!" Marcus said shaking his head, grateful for the jokey banter he had been missing these past few months.

"Where's Rachel? How is she?" Freddo asked good naturedly. Marcus looked across to the aisle in the far corner of the shop and pointed with his head. "She's over there getting some baby gear. Yeh she's fine, bit tired but that comes with the territory, I guess."

Rachel was busy looking at feeding bottles. The double buggy was close by containing the peacefully sleeping boys oblivious to the world outside. Gazing across from a distance, he took stock of her small frame as she blended in with the other mothers in the store. What had happened to the chic, stylish woman he'd fallen in love with ten years earlier.

Her fine blonde hair hung limply in soft strands but badly needed a restyle and cut, the over-sized jacket a legacy from her pregnancy, carefully continued to hide her extra layers and trainers were something she previously would never have worn outside the gym.

Rachel knew she was losing control but did not know how to regain it. These shopping trips with Marcus were an assemblance of married life that helped her feel that things were alright generally. From an outsider's perspective there they were, the perfect married couple. Her husband dutifully going shopping, waiting patiently for her.

Then they would grab a quick perfectly made organic coffee, and she would feed the twins in the welcoming atmosphere amongst other yummy mummies; then home, and they would spend the afternoon playing with the boys and doing lovely family things together. Wrong.

Rewind to two hours earlier. She'd been up since six o'clock trying to keep up with the growing feeding requirements of the twins who seemed to have an endless need for milk. Marcus was fast asleep oblivious to the cacophony of noise in the kitchen coming from the kettle, microwave, radio and baby wails.

After this shop, they would go to the local coffee house down the road and sit silently avoiding eye contact and exchanging babies. Same day, different perspective she thought, looking furtively across the aisle at other mothers and husbands looking at baby paraphernalia.

Suddenly she felt an urge to put something in the pram. Without much thought and effort to conceal her actions, she took a bottle and some feeder cups and put them under the baby blanket. There. Shopping done.

She moved to another aisle and headed casually towards the door. "Excuse me madam, can I take a look inside your pram please?" A store detective dressed like a shopper said politely blocking the doorway. "No of course not!" Rachel retorted, "Who are you and why would I allow a stranger to look under my babies' blanket" she continued heatedly. "Please, can we go into the office madam." The woman said with more authority this time. "What office? And what are you talking about?" Rachel said, beginning to sound upset. "You can't just go around intimidating people!".

Marcus, vaguely aware of what seemed to be the beginning of a fracas in the shop, looked up from his conversation and glanced across to what appeared to be his wife, and another shopper. The woman seemed to be trying to lead Rachel somewhere and a small crowd of shoppers were beginning to nod and nudge each other. 'What the fu..' He suddenly realised that Rachel was involved and made his way into the shop. "Rachel, what's happened, what's wrong? He said urgently as she threw herself into his arms.

"I'm afraid we've found some products in your wife's possession that have not been paid for." They made their way into the small office at the back of the shop whilst the store detective began to take notes and ask a series of questions. Name, address, telephone number, why were the products in the pram? Did she know she was on CCTV? The value of the items totalled £29,99, their policy on shop lifters, and prosecution, and so it went on. Marcus knew they were out of their depth and that also, Rachel's behaviour was not about stealing, but more about getting attention.

He walked to a corner of the room for privacy and texted Carrie. "Cass I/we need you. Rachel's been done for shoplifting in Mothercare. I'm with her now but don't know what to do. Please…x" A response pinged its way back by the magic of technology immediately. "I'll be there in 20 luckily I'm working from home. X"

Carrie was a breath of fresh air as she walked into the room half an hour later, calm and smiling assuredly. She had spent ten minutes previously with the Store Manager and had managed to persuade him that post-natal depression had caused the unusual behaviour change in her friend, whilst offering to pay for everything immediately.

Rachel's watery eyes smiled gratefully as a wave of shame took over her and released a flood of tears. Marcus took in Carrie's beauty and had to stop himself from kissing her. Instead, he squeezed her hand gently when Rachel was attending to the boys.

There was no need for thanks. The tender knowing touch was enough, Carrie knew that. Feeling the familiar slim fingers slip into hers was comforting, reassuring, but also the covertness, sexy. Their eyes met briefly in acknowledgement and then it was over, and the moment passed.

Chapter 16

Hattie

Hattie walked into the staff room after the half term break taking in the glances up and down from certain colleagues who had noticed her increasing flamboyance and buoyant attitude. She tried to keep the grin off her face and transferred it to a smile, feeling that this was more composed, given the fact that she was bursting with excitement inside. She had made a real effort this morning as she confidently strode across the busy room strewn with papers on low tables alongside coffee mugs and laptops.

The tight striped trousers complemented a loose-fitting black cashmere sweater, ankle boots and a messy hair top knot. These days she had begun to spend more money on quality and less on quantity where clothes were concerned following Francoise's style.

She glanced down at her watch – 8.35am, only two hours before she was going to be there to talk to her students about choosing degree subjects and entering university.

She sat down slightly breathless and began to go through her lesson plans for the week. "You're very bright eyed and bushy tailed for a Monday morning," observed Joe her colleague and secret guilty pleasure that somehow, she had never quite fathomed out why.

His wavy dark hair and smiling eyes had something to do with it, which is probably why she had never mentioned to Rob if they went out for the odd drink after work to let off steam about the day, the week, the month. She shrugged nonchalantly and winked "I've had a good half term."

"And?" he questioned further. Choosing to deflect his question, she smiled again, "Joe I've got to go, I've got a class in five minutes and then I've got to meet Francoise Hubert who is coming to do the Sixth Form seminar on university choices." "Ah I see, I've moved down the pecking order and out of the circle of trust!" he responded good humouredly.

Hattie's cheeks flushed as she gathered her things hoping that he hadn't noticed. "Not at all! Frankie is a dear friend who I met during the school Paris trip. I told you about her."

"Oh, Frankie is it now?" he persisted. "Shut up Joe," Hattie said meeting his eyes knowingly, trying to ignore the butterflies in her stomach.

She didn't like lying to Rob but Hattie wanted Francoise to herself that evening. They sat in the corner of the quiet bistro around the corner from her house sipping wine. Francoise's hand brushed Hattie's as she gently entwined her fingers briefly until pulling away. "There's an opening in Cambridge for a part time lecturer, why don't you apply?" She said locking eyes.

176

Hattie looked down wondering why her heart was beating so quickly. "What? I can't do that. And any way I'd have no chance."

"You're more than qualified babe. Why don't you just look at what their looking for and see? You know you've always wanted to do something like that."

"Frankie I can't just leave my life here and take off to Cambridge! What about my family, my kids? Life isn't as simple as you think you know." The nickname coined by Hattie was regularly used as a term of endearment and gave intimacy to their discussion.

"It can be though Hattie. It's all about choices and what makes you happy. Cambridge isn't the other end of the world, right? It's an hour from London. Why don't you just take a look and see where it takes you? Don't think about the consequences or logistics right now." She smiled and leaned in towards her conspiratorially, "Can you imagine being able to see each other all the time," she whispered, as she took Hattie's hand and squeezed it gently. Unknown to Hattie, a seed had been planted, and like a flower that unfurls, with careful watering and nurturing, it was to bloom and flourish if only for a while.

Carrie

It was difficult to avoid Marcus, given Rachel's recent ordeal in Mothercare. As much as she did not want to, Carrie found herself on the doorstep crossing her fingers that Marcus would not be there.

She knocked gently just in case the twins were asleep and hoped that Rachel would hurry up. Marcus opened the door unshaven, wearing a pair of worn jeans and a checked lumberjack shirt with a T-shirt underneath that read #bored. "Hi gorgeous," he smiled sheepishly as he stood back to let Carrie in. "The criminal's upstairs," he said gesturing. "Stop it Marcus," she said nudging him, as she stepped into the kitchen. "How are things?" she asked gently as she took the lead and put the kettle on. "As well as can be expected, I guess.

She spends most of the day upstairs apart from coming down for a tea every now and then but at least we're not arguing" he shrugged, leaning against the kitchen work top.

Carrie busied herself getting mugs out of the cupboard, trying to not get flustered as she hadn't been in such close proximity to Marcus since the evening, they had in a bar back in the summer. This wasn't supposed to happen.

Up until this year, they had managed to avoid each other all year, but things had taken a different course these past few months. He walked over behind her and gently brushed her arm, "I've missed you so much Cass," he whispered into her hair.

She moved quickly to one side, heart beating wildly, choosing to ignore him. "I'll take Rachel a cup," she said forcing a nonchalant smile. "Sure, yes, go ahead she's looking forward to seeing you," he said stepping away picking up the signal to back off.

Carrie followed the sounds of baby squeals and muffled conversation between Rachel and her boys and walked up the stairs slowly with a heavy heart. The guilt and emotional turmoil fluttered within her stomach as she carefully turned the door handle and peeped into the room. "Hi hun," she whispered to Rachel who was leaning against the bedhead tickling the boys as they lay next to her gurgling. She smiled back wanly and patted the bed gesturing. Carrie sat down carefully and squeezed her hand gently, "So how's it going? Are you feeling better?"

"I'm ok Cass," she responded unconvincingly. "Do you want to tell me about it?" Carrie pressed. "There's nothing to tell. It's just something I like doing. I'm not sure why."

"Did you want to be caught?"

"What? No of course not!" She hesitated and considered her answer again. "Yes! Yes, I did," Rachel said after a moment. The cry for help had been quietly screaming inside her for months.

She shrugged tiredly and gestured to the wardrobe. "Take a look. I could most probably open a shop on eBay." Carrie walked over to the large, fitted, wardrobe and slid the door to one side. "What an earth? Rachel how the hell did you ever get a giant panda out the door?" She peered in more closely and rummaged through a Mothercare bag. "Why did you take trainer pants? The boys are 8 weeks old!" Her mouth twitched as she tried to hide a smile that seemed to come from nowhere.

Rachel's eye met Carrie's gaze as the friends began laughing at the absurdity of the situation. "In case we got invaded by Russians?" she said laughing.

"Or is it because Brexit will result in a nappy crisis" Carrie guffawed. She fell on to the bed holding her sides as the stress of the last ten months released them both. Each time they tried to talk, laughter took over with tears of relief and delight rolled down their cheeks. "I particularly liked the double G bra as well," Rachel screeched. "What to hold Marcus's footballs?" Carrie roared.

Marcus hearing the commotion ran up the stairs and opened the door. Rachel and Carrie lay across the bed with the contents of the wardrobe strewn haphazardly across the bed and floor, leaving just enough room for the boys who continued gurgling contentedly. "What an earth?" he said looking at the ensuing chaos. "What?! It'll all come in useful one day Marcus," Rachel said laughing again.

Marcus hadn't seen or heard Rachel laugh for months and remembered for a split second why he had fallen in love with her all those years ago. He shook his head and looked at Carrie for a better explanation.

She gathered up the twins in her arms and carefully handed them to him. "Here, they're ready for a feed, I think. We'll clear up and come down ok," she whispered, as she gently closed the door behind him and threw herself back on the bed laughing with Rachel once more.

Jenna

Jenna searched through her wardrobe trying to find something suitable to wear. She needed to look professional but not formal, although she wasn't even sure why she had agreed to meet with her former boss after an email that he had sent a few days before.

The cryptic note didn't reveal much, other than a friendly "how are you" and it would be good to meet if she had time, there was something he would like to discuss." It was sufficiently vague to appeal to her curiosity to want to find out more, and now three days later she found herself considering pulling out, although deep inside she was also excited at the prospect of having lunch in the city.

A suit was too formal these days, a shift dress, a bit staid, eventually settling for a smart casual look with skinny jeans, ankle boots, crisp white shirt and designer tailored jacket, a legacy from her old career. Her carefully moussed "bed head" hair gave her an air of nonchalance, sass even, she considered, as she put the finishing touches to her makeup and looked around for her oversized designer bag.

The hour journey reminded Jenna why she had given up her high-flying career. However, stepping off the train on to the busy platform at Marylebone, she fell into a familiar and easy walk, weaving her way through commuters, feeling a forgotten sense of fulfilment and optimism.

The cold crisp November air brought a freshness and purity to the day as the morning sun filtered through the cloud and bounced off the glass architecture in London's financial district. She crossed the busy street heading towards Liverpool Street, keeping a look out for their old haunt Café Columbo, a trendy café bar discreetly tucked between two office blocks.

As she approached the café, a familiar self-doubt crept into her psyche making her feel increasingly nervous "pull yourself together Jen" she told herself "It's not as if he found a cracking error in last years' figures before I left". The thought left her clammy with sweat. A small bead of perspiration trickled down the side of her forehead as she gently pushed open the glass door and walked in looking around.

Tom Bradbury stood up in recognition smiling as he nodded in acknowledgement and gestured towards Jenna to join him. His navy suit emanated wealth as did the discreet gold cuff links and silk tie. Jenna walked towards him relaxing as he opened his arms and hugged her with genuine fondness. "My my, you've got younger, I must say.

Is that what leaving this business does to you?" he said as they sat down. He placed an order for breakfast and winked, "I take it that our usual brekkie is still OK with you?" Jenna blushed and nodded still trying to get her head into gear. Ever since she had left this world it seemed as if her brain had gone to porridge she contemplated.

Laughter came easily over reminiscing and anecdotes. Jenna relaxed, and continued to wait for the news that she was in trouble. She half listened to Tom's voice as he explained the ups and downs of the business and the new graduate in-take. "So, what do you think?" he said looking at her. "What do I think of what?" she replied confused. "Jen, you haven't been listening to me. The proposal I've just put on the table," he said exasperated. "Are you talking about the Graduate Training Scheme? I'm sure Jack or Susan would be able to take that on," she said absentmindedly. "I want you. Figuratively speaking of course," he smiled. "Huh?" She sat up abruptly with the slow realisation that he was talking about her. "Just to clarify, you want me to head up the firm's graduate trainee scheme?"

"Yes. You'd be perfect for it and I've negotiated a 4-day week for you so that you can still do your flower growing stuff."

"Well, that's very presumptuous Tom," she said huffily. "And I don't just grow flowers thank you very much. In fact, I might not be able to manage 4 days as I'm so busy," she said lying. "However, I think I might still be able to help you out," she continued, as her heart began to beat faster.

"I thought you might," he said, knowing that he was doing her a favour as much as she was him. "Shall we discuss terms later in the week and I can get a contract drawn up." Jenna squeezed her friend's hand, "Yes let's do that," she said, putting on her jacket as her heart began to sing.

Chapter 17

Hattie

"I've often wondered if adultery runs in the genes, like blue eyes or buck teeth. Am I unfaithful because it's written in my DNA?" ("The Infidelity Chain" – Tess Stimson)

Hattie read through her CV one last time and then reviewed the carefully crafted cover letter and pressed "send". She wasn't quite sure if the guilt she felt was about the fact that she had actually gone ahead, and applied for the job in Cambridge, or more that lying to her husband and friends, had seemingly become a serial habit these days.

She reasoned with herself, after all it wasn't lying as such, but rather being economical with the truth. The two days a week in Cambridge lecturing in art history was something that she had never considered possible, until Francoise had convinced her that she had a real chance. The reckless side of Hattie hidden in the deep recess of her mind, pushed her to put the application in without heed of the consequences.

The dynamic between the group wasn't quite the same without Rachel that evening. She had backed down at the last minute as the twins both had colds leaving the remaining three friends to hunker down and drink the obligatory inner sanctum wine together.

Twenty five percent of input, twenty five percent of innuendo, twenty five percent of soul searching was missing but somehow a different intimacy took its place where Hattie, Jenna and Carrie had no-one to hide behind or dominate the conversation.

An uncomfortable silence hovered between the three friends when the opening lines of the book were read aloud by Jenna. "So, anyone want to start?" she said looking across to the others.

Carrie responded by using the controversy tactic to divert attention. "Everyone's capable of adultery I'm sure," she said, pausing to take note of the exchange of glances across the table. She continued, "I suppose no-one knows if they are capable until they find themselves in a situation that might result in it."

"You think it's ok, do you?" Jenna asked pointedly. "I didn't say that. I just meant that one doesn't know if one's capable of adultery until a situation occurs and you react in a particular way, but you would never know how you might feel or react at the time."

"Is it adultery if you have thoughts but don't go through with it?" Jenna asked to no-one in particular.

"What do you mean? That just having thoughts about being with somebody else is also unfaithfulness? You can't control your thoughts surely?"

Hattie said defensively. Jenna's blank face led to further discourse as Hattie continued unable to stop herself. "Of course, it isn't," said Hattie. She was about to continue with an explanation that it was about having sex with someone who isn't a married partner and then stopped herself.

"What if somebody has an affair with somebody who's married but they aren't? That could be perceived as not adultery from their point of view, couldn't it?" Jenna responded heatedly.

"Guys, let's not get too het up over this shall we?" Said Carrie. "It is only chick lit after all, not exactly deep and meaningful prose, is it?" hoping to deflect the conversation.

"I think it's quite a controversial opener actually. But it does beg the question if this is something that is more prone to men than women? And if this is this a man or a woman's point of view," Jenna mused. The discussion between the differences between the sexes continued until they reached an impasse. Secretly each one of the friends was grateful that their behaviours outside the circle of trust hadn't been exposed.

Not knowing where to take the conversation next, Jenna's random monologue, triggered by two large glasses of wine took Hattie and Cassie by surprise. "So, you'll never guess what," she said, filling up their glasses. "What?" said Cassie sipping slowly, wondering what was going to come up next. "I'm going back into the city and kick starting my career again would you believe?"

Hattie and Carrie looked at each other in wonder and simultaneously got out of their chairs and hugged Jenna with genuine fondness and relief for her. "Good for you girl!" Carrie said playfully ruffling Jenna's short pixie haircut. "Well as we're in the mood for sharing, I might as well tell you that I've also applied for a job," Hattie confessed, looking around to judge the reaction. "Wow, where, what, when?" Carrie asked interested and grateful that the conversation had taken a different path.

"I'm not saying, it probably won't get anywhere," she replied sending a signal to the other two that she was not prepared to say anything further. In fact. Hattie wasn't sure why she had said something in the first place. Now that she had told them, it was official. She had officially put it out there that her life might change but none of them realised just how much.

Chapter 18

December

"The thing about people is that it takes years, and years, and years to know them. Really know them. Because we hide things, all of us, all the time. We're ashamed, cautious or secretive. Sometimes, we just have trust issues and feel people need to earn the right to knowledge about our true selves. We don't gift it generously. And even when you finally think you know someone, something changes. We can't know each other. It's a fool's game trying to." ("Lies Lies Lies" – Adele Parks)

<u>Carrie</u>

It was a sure sign that the year was drawing to a close when emails had started to come into Carrie's inbox about the office Christmas party. She sighed and rooted in her handbag for her phone to check once again if Ben had texted her. Still no sign.

She figured that this feeling inside that she hadn't quite been able to fathom was indeed, loneliness, something that she had experienced since she was five years old and when her dad had left her and her mother alone, without any explanation.

Despite her young age, she had always felt an uneasy gap in her heart which she had never quite been able to fill. Instead, as she grew older and entered adulthood, she concentrated on her career, deciding that she would never let a man get that close to her again.

The closest thing that had come to it was her friendship with Marcus and that wasn't based on the sex. Carrie had a deep connection with him which had started more than ten years before when Rachel brought him along to a party one New Year's Eve.

She replayed the moment in her head as Rachel bounced into the room pulling a handsome male behind her by the hand beaming with happiness. The brief flicker of acknowledgement in the smile of his eyes told her "You seem nice, I like you and I'd like to get to know you better," even though no words were spoken between them.

Later as the evening wore on, as people got up on the dance floor and they were left standing by the bar, their humour bounced off each other as they observed the array of fancy dress around the room. "So why didn't you come in fancy dress then?" she asked.

"Well, I wanted to come as a pantomime horse, but I couldn't persuade Rachel to have her head up my backside all evening and thinking about it, we've only known each other 2 months after all," he said shrugging. "What about you?" He said turning towards her to top up her glass. "Well, when you get to know me better, you'll find out that I'm always late, forget everything, and last to know about details, like the fact that it was a fancy-dress party."

He smiled "Interesting. What kind of person is always late, forgets details, and is the last to know about everything?"

"A criminal lawyer!" she said laughing at the absurdity of it. "I'll have to remember to never have you as my brief," he said laughing. And so, the banter continued for years at dinner parties, pub get togethers, with partners, and of course, the obligatory New Year's Eve when they always came together and celebrated as a group.

It was five years earlier when things changed, and Carrie's life became more complicated.

That night, the cold, crystal clear black sky was littered with stars and breath became a whisper of smoke that got lost in the dark when a word was uttered, she recalled. The crisp night was almost identical to the one where she had met Ben and bumped his car. Five hours of champagne and dinner had taken its toll as the gang had slowly sunk into sofas in Rachel's lounge after bringing in the New Year. Hattie and Rachel were asleep, and their men were talking and listening to music, Jenna curled on the floor at Jack's knee.

Marcus was in the garden having a sneaky cigarette, a habit he had supposedly managed to stop. Carrie strolled outside and breathed in the crisp air. "So here we are again," he said smiling. She shivered in the cold, "I'm not a fan of New Year's Eve actually," she said. "Now you tell me! And there's me thinking that you love it, you do a pretty good job of hiding it."

He opened his coat and gestured to her. "Come here, you're freezing." She hesitated for a moment and went towards him as he wrapped the coat around them taking in the stars above. The innocent gesture had no intent behind it and was done purely instinctively as a friend. But fate took its course as the two locked eyes and kissed. Hidden by the trees and privacy of the large shrubs they continued unable to stop, breathless, passionate, and urgent. Finally, when the moment was over their sobriety told them never to speak of it until of course it was to happen again, one year to the day the following year.

She knew it had to stop and grappled with the increasing guilt as the weak December sun filtered through the office window and the year was beginning to end as quickly as it had begun. For the first time in years, she was trying to think of a suitable excuse to back out of the New Year's Eve get together but struggled to find one. She did not deserve to be happy she reasoned with herself, after all how could she when she had been living a life of deception for the past five years.

As if by telepathy her phone bleeped signalling a message. She glanced down at her phone, ignoring the growing number of emails that needed a response, unable to concentrate. "So, are we all Ok for NYE?" The group text pinged from Jenna. "Wondered about doing something a bit different. Fancy going out girls only first and then go out to a club or something with the rest later?" Ping! Ping! Ping! The favourable responses from the others came soon after.

Carrie hesitated, giving herself space to think. She didn't have time to come up with an alternative scenario for herself that might seem plausible. What the hell, she texted back, "Yeh sure, I'm in," and sat back, she would come up with something later, there was at least three weeks to sort something else out.

Another text came through. What the hell, she opened it without looking at the sender. "Hi Cass, I know it's been a hard year and that we need to stop this. One last time? I miss talking to you. Please?" Marcus pressed send and crossed his fingers not sure what the response might be.

Rachel

"She didn't want to be a beauty queen, but as luck would have it, she was about to become one" ("Funny Girl" – Nick Hornby)

Rachel packaged up the last of the trainer pants, milk products and baby clothes and sealed the brown card box with packing tape. She carefully wrote the store name and address and headed to the car boot. The twins were safely in their car seats cooing and playing with their toes.

Things had changed since Carrie had come over and put some perspective on her life. Finally, the bubble she had been living in had burst and a ray of light had begun to shine through. She was on her way to the post office to send back the paraphernalia she had taken and mark the start of her journey back to planet normality. Later that day she was about to interview the nanny who Marcus had finally persuaded her to have, something that she had been completely averse to for months.

The local high street shops twinkled with fairy lights and Christmas trees. Steamy windows beckoned shoppers to take a closer look at their contents and excited toddlers held their mother's hands jumping up and down excitedly. Rachel pushed the double buggy manoeuvring through crowds as her spirit started to soar. The feeling was unusual and something that she hadn't recognised for months, if not years, suddenly hope lingered in the air.

She stopped in front of a small shop front with modern art strategically placed next to a Christmas tree festooned in pink lights and feathers. Hanging off one of the branches was a small sign written in fluorescent pink with the words, "We're Hiring!". As if on automatic pilot she pushed open the door and walked in peering around. "Hi, can I help you?" A voice emerged from behind a computer.

The man in his thirties wearing a loose black sweater and jeans looked up from his clear Perspex desk in the corner of the room. His face, hidden by the large flat screen emerged when he stood up smiling. His dark hair touched the nape of his neck; tortoise shell glasses slipped down the bridge of his nose. He took the glasses off his face and tucked them into the neckline of the cashmere sweater he was wearing waiting for a response.

Rachel felt frumpy and mumsy in the minimalist décor and varnished wooden floor. Acutely aware of the babies and cumbersome buggy, she responded, "I saw from your window that you're recruiting staff? I have a degree in art and graphics and have managed galleries before?" she said trailing off.

"Great! Do you have a CV? It's part-time but it may move to full time after about 6 months. If you leave your CV, I'll pass it on to the manager."

Rachel hadn't updated her CV in nearly 12 months. She quickly scribbled her email, phone number and LinkedIn profile on a piece of paper in her handbag. "I can get a CV to you in a few days, but you might want to look at LinkedIn in the meantime," she said, not quite knowing where her gall had come from.

"Sure, will do," he said smiling. Rachel turned tail and walked out of the door waving before she had a chance to back down and tell him it was complete fabrication. Her LinkedIn profile looked good, but in reality, she had been a new mum on the verge of a breakdown for the past few months, not a high-flying Arts Administrator, capable of buying and selling art for wealthy individuals. Her cheeks burned and a rush of heat went through her as she pushed the door open with the buggy and went into the cold crisp air outside.

What had she done, was she mad, she contemplated as she continued walking to the post office. By the time she had reached her destination, she had convinced herself that it would never come to anything anyway and put the impromptu moment to the back of her mind. One thing at a time Rachel she breathed as she pushed the parcel through the glass window for posting, the first step towards putting the past few months behind her.

Marcus was pouring tea into a mug when she walked back into the kitchen with the boys in her arms. She smiled and handed him one taking the mug. "You've been busy," he said, cuddling the baby catching Rachel's eye.

"What?" she asked eying him up and down.

"Didn't realise that you were job hunting today," he said. Rachel could not read his face which seemed expressionless. "How do you know that? And no, I have not been job hunting, what are you talking about? She responded confused.

"Some guy phoned asking for you. Said something about you enquiring about a vacancy at a gallery in the high street?" he said, eyebrows raised inquisitively.

Open mouthed, her gaping mouth moved to explain but the continuous ring tone on her mobile distracted her. She handed the baby in her arms to Marcus and answered still flustered. "Rachel Welbeck?" A deep low voice asked. "Yes, that's me," she answered whilst shrugging her shoulders to Marcus. The voice continued, "I'm sorry to call you out of the blue but I'm calling from Bespoke Arts. You spoke to a colleague of mine this afternoon enquiring about a job here." Rachel didn't respond, still reeling from the shock.

"Hi, are you still there?" he asked. Not waiting for the response, he continued, "I know you were going to send in a CV, but I've taken the liberty of looking at your LinkedIn profile and wondered if we might meet informally to discuss the position?" She looked at Marcus who could hear some of the conversation, he nodded to her encouragingly. And there it was. Fate had turned its course and the stars had finally aligned as she found herself slowly agreeing to meet the next day.

Hattie

Hattie waited outside the Board room in the faculty of arts at one of the colleges in Cambridge. She was nervous and almost regretted agreeing to the interview. Yet more lies had ensued. Lies at school, lies to Rob, lies to the girls. She seemed to be lying to everybody these days, perhaps including herself she mused.

She caught sight of herself in the tinted glass wall of the meeting room and looked at the sophisticated designer suit, sharp jimmy choo heels and designer bag. What had she become? was this her or was she lying to herself? she couldn't decide She glanced again at her reflection, the only concession to her individuality was her T-shirt. The slogan jumped out at her "Stay True". What was she doing here? she questioned her decision to come once again.

She looked at her watch, another fifteen minutes or so before she was due to go in. The last candidate had been in there for over an hour, and she could hear muffled voices and the odd laughter.

The job description certainly reflected her career path; degree in Fine Art from a Russel Group university, tick; Master's in art history, tick; minimum ten years teaching experience, tick; specialist area art and gender, tick.

Desirable skills: ability to supervise practical portfolios, tick; fluent Italian, almost tick; published work, tick, well at least her dissertation was published she told herself. She continued looking at the job spec reading it, carefully taking in the ethos and the nuances of the person the university was looking for. She knew that if she really wanted it, she had a good chance of being short-listed at the very least, but doubt lingered inside her.

The life decision ahead, unnerved her and presented a future that would affect not just her but her husband, children, friends, and colleagues. Ten minutes. Stay true Hattie she said to herself as she buttoned her jacket and walked out of the foyer.

Jenna

Jenna was on fire. She had just finished her first day back in the office and her head was buzzing. She had forgotten the adrenalin rush she got from being back in the fast-moving environment of London's financial district.

She was a woman in a male dominated environment and had earned her credibility on merit alone. She recalled how she fell into an easy dialogue with her graduate trainees and the feeling of respect she felt from those who knew her background and credentials. Finally, after twelve months of struggle she was beginning to feel in control of herself and her life.

She was tired of the lies. Tired of the pretence to Jack. Tired of the pretence to herself that she was struggling without him.

She wanted her friends, her children, her colleagues, mums at the school gate, the woman at the checkout in Sainsburys, her husband, to see the independent, happy-

198

go-lucky person she was. The one who people envy and wish their life was like hers. The truth was that Jenna's smile masked the doubt and fear that she had held deep inside since going it alone.

It wasn't a real lie she told herself, merely an interpretation of the truth.

The professional career woman, the glam mum with the handsome sons, the thriving business, the long-time friends, the mature trial separation that enabled her to remain friends with her husband.

She looked around the chaotic lounge realising that the only person who really knew her was Jack, not Rachel, not Hattie, not Cass but her still husband who she could fall asleep in front of, who saw the lines on her face, and the history behind those lines, who knew when she was lying, who knew when she was scared, and who knew when she was struggling.

Why had he suggested the split, albeit temporary she considered, doubt creeping into her psyche again – did he really know her? Did she really know him? Everybody has secrets. Secrets that cover the fear, the uncertainty, the love, the hate, the equilibrium, the jealousy, the regret, and the hope that it will get better.

Chapter 19

<u>Carrie</u>

Carrie was playing a dangerous game of emotional chess. One where she was heading towards check mate if she made the wrong decision over what to do next. Playing games was not Carrie's style.

She believed she had more integrity, but she was being pulled in different directions emotionally and psychologically which made decisions even more difficult. She desperately needed it to end it with Marcus but knew that he genuinely needed a friend and had no-one to turn to. Equally, the feelings that had surfaced for Ben had come unexpectedly as she increasingly missed seeing him and felt a pang of longing.

She texted back, "OK one last time but that's it, Marcus you know that" ping. Immediate response. "That's fantastic. I completely understand Cass. Maybe we go to eat then see how it goes? I'm booked into the Hilton Park Lane." "Just dinner," she texted back tersely. "Yeh sure. Soz," came the reply. "8pm in the restaurant and don't be late." Carrie's text pinged back as she turned to her mounting paperwork.

She knew she was being unfair but couldn't help herself. The familiar feelings of confusion and anger rose inside as the returning guilt and emotional seesaw that had dominated her life, since New Year's Eve five years before, grappled with her conscience.

Since then, she had never been able to find somebody who fulfilled her and made her complete in the way Marcus did.

And whilst they only had one day each year, it seemed to fill the gap in her life that she had lived with since university and which was replaced by her second love of law. Whilst Carrie's friends fell into a familiar pattern of career, marriage, and babies, she continued to make her way up the career ladder without the distractions and divergence of men and family. She quietly buried the longing to share her life with somebody and have the family she never had as a child and focused on helping others through her work.

Sitting in the South African sunshine, she looked up at Thabo and smiled weakly. "I don't know what Ben has told you, but I really like him. It's the first time I've felt a connection with somebody for a long, long time. The trouble is, I'm not the person he thinks I am. I've done something that I'm not proud of and I don't deserve him. That's why I said we shouldn't continue seeing each other."

Thabo's face was hard to read as he studied the serious eyes that searched his face for a clue to his feelings. "We all do things that we regret. Ben hasn't said much to me, only that he had met an amazing woman; it was only while you were talking that I realised it was you."

Carrie remembered the drunken fumble with Marcus in the darkness on New Year's Eve five years before. Why did it happen, and more to the point, why had she allowed it to happen she wondered? Her moral compass was usually set very high, and it was incongruous to her nature and principles to betray any woman, let alone a close friend.

She shuddered quietly inside as the guilt rose in her stomach like fluttering feathers, making her feel slightly sick. The connection with Marcus had always been strong and somehow a natural instinctive urge had taken over that evening between them, where they couldn't stop themselves from showing their feelings to each other.

Feelings that had kept submerged for years and that they had separately fought to control. Every year after, they made a pact to never meet again but as the year came to a close, it was a decision that they could not adhere to.

Thabo smiled at her showing warmth in his eyes. "Don't give yourself such a hard time Carrie. I know Ben would rather be with you than anyone else. This might be your time you know?"

"How can you be so forgiving?"

"I've had six months to myself remember. When you're left alone with your thoughts, it's easy to see things more clearly and get a perspective on things. Life is too short, I guess."

"I need to learn from you," Carrie said smiling back in awe. There was something about this person that held a deep wisdom about him, an emotional intelligence that cut through the waffle with clarity and perspective.

"Come on, let's go and get drunk! It's about time I showed you some of the best places in Joburg." He shrugged pushing back his chair as he stood up offering his hand. She allowed him to pull her up, feeling the burden that had been sitting on her shoulders, lighten, unaware that Ben was propping up the bar listening to the conversation.

***

Carrie stepped off the plane and turned up the collar of her wool Ralph Lauren coat. There was a biting wind sweeping across the tarmac and the grey sky that welcomed her back on to terra firma solid ground was the complete antithesis of her time in South Africa. The long plane journey had given her time to process the conversation with Thabo resulting in an epiphany moment of clarity.

Reflecting on his words 'This might be your time you know.' She contemplated his wisdom and ability to forgive, wondering if forgiveness could be innate in everybody – perhaps Ben might be able to forgive her if he were ever to find out. She had committed a crime against friendship, a crime against loyalty, and a crime against a sense of common humanity that unites people of all nations.

Adultery was not a crime in the true sense of the word, but it was unacceptable, illicit behaviour, that rarely had cause for genuine empathy. As a growing fear of losing Ben began to gnaw at her brain, she realised that she had to do something quickly.

She fished around in the bag under her seat and found the worn notebook and pen which would pen her darkest thoughts. She hesitated and wrote 'Dear Marcus' no! Too formal, unfamiliar, distant 'Hello Marcus' No, too casual, unimportant. In the end she started the letter she has been putting off for weeks, 'Marcus'.

'Words in a conversation seem too transient for what I need to say. They can be lost in the mist of time, conveniently forgotten, or a twisted memory that recalls only what one wants to hear.

Forgive me for the formality of putting my words on paper but I need to write them down to release me from the guilt of betrayal that I, (and both of us) have been living with for the past 5 years. We always said that we would never talk about our feelings; that each year, it would be the last; that this 'secret' would never creep into our 'other' lives.

But here we are, heading towards New Year and still being pulled towards seeing each other. This time though, you are a dad, you have responsibilities in more ways than one, and, by some great fortune and serendipity, I have met Ben, and found somebody I realise now that I want to be with; spend my life with; grow old with.' My behaviour doesn't warrant good luck and because of this, I always thought that I would never find anyone, but I don't want to lose this chance now.'

Carrie knew that the timing of the letter and Marcus's willingness to accept its contents and process it was crucial. She quickly glanced inside her bag as she stepped off the plane, double checking that it remained, covertly hidden amongst the usual paraphernalia of her bag, until she felt ready to send it, discreetly typed, in a brown envelope as if an invoice from a supplier.

Chapter 20

<u>New Year's Eve</u>

"Our every intended action, in a sense our whole life – how we choose to live it within the context of limitations imposed by our circumstances – can be seen as our answer to the great question that confronts us all. "How am I to be happy?" ("Ancient Wisdom, Modern World" – Dalai Lama)

Carrie's nerves left a feeling of nausea in her stomach as she got ready for the evening celebration. She had lost weight and the black sequinned dress that she wore hung loosely across her body. Her willowy silhouette displayed toned shoulders and arms which had benefited from regular strength training and boxing. She slipped on her statement heels and dabbed perfume on her wrist and neck glancing at her phone to check the time. She was meeting the girls as planned for cocktails and somehow as luck would have it, for the first time in years they had decided to each do their own thing later in the evening.

Reflecting on the course of the year, it was a marker to each of them that things had changed, and an unspoken acceptance lingered that made it disagreeable to ask each other the detail of what they were doing afterwards.

Her phone bleeped again. The text from Marcus was bordering on needy if she didn't know him better. Slightly irritated she ignored his impatience and texted back an emoji of a girl shrugging then turned off her phone.

Rachel, Hattie, and Jenna were about to start their second cocktail as Carrie entered the busy Soho bar which was buzzing from New Year's Eve excitement. The crowded room was festooned with fairy lights that twinkled gaily in the large opulent mirrors and glass chandeliers that hung from the high ceilings. Italian statues gilded in gold and bronze gave the bar a feeling of opulence and decadence of the nineteen thirties. A series of discreet booths took up one side of the room and complemented the large round tables covered in crisp white linen and gold cutlery for those who were eating.

She stood in the doorway and took in the atmosphere as she looked around for the gang. Her eye fell upon three women laughing together, huddled in a booth on the far side of the room. Slightly removed from the situation, Carrie observed her closest friends from afar and acknowledged how much they had all changed. Like a phoenix rising from the ashes, each of them had tackled their own challenges and demonstrated a resilience of the human spirit that made her heart soar; they were so much better than her. Jenna with her new pixie hair cut had returned to her career in the city with an air of quiet confidence that showed itself in her demeanour, her clothes. And her choice to remain single for the time being. She was having too much of a good time in the city to want to return to the routine of marriage. This change of heart seemed to have attracted Jack back into her life but this time it was Jenna calling the shots not him.

Hattie was wiping a tear from her eye as she cried with laughter. No doubt her stories were keeping the other two amused Carrie thought, as she continued to observe from afar. The unruly mane of red curls and Hattie's signature look took Carrie back to those early student days when she was known as the pied piper, continuously meeting new friends and connecting people together.

Hattie had started painting again and was putting together a portfolio for an exhibition. Her talent was obvious, and its latent re-emergence was the catalyst for her giving up her job to focus full time on her art. Could that be down to her new friend she wondered. It seemed that since meeting her back in April on a school trip to Paris, the old Hattie had come back with a vengeance. Two stones lighter than last New Year's Eve, Hattie was a different person physically, emotionally, and mentally. Gone were the baggy, frumpy hide all dresses and in were the narrow-striped trousers, heels and cropped top that showed off her perfectly flat belly. Whilst her career had taken a new path, her relationship still had a way to go, but hey you can't get everything right in one go right, Carrie considered.

And then there was Rachel. Sweet, unassuming, Rachel who had struggled for years with understanding who she really was as a person. For so long she had tried to be the daughter, wife, and mother she longed to be, but even then, she struggled to remember who she was before she had been with Marcus. The woman who loved art, was good at business management, and capable of doing anything she wanted, had slowly disappeared. She had put all her energy into having a baby whilst her marriage became increasingly fragmented and weak, or had it? More secrets, more economy with the truth. Their marriage was strong, they had worked so hard to have a baby and through all of this, Marcus stood by Rachel.

Carrie tried to excuse herself for the situation she had created, finally accepting that like a spider to a fly, it was she who had enticed Marcus when he was at his lowest ebb and created a web of deceit. A convenient omission of the truth and something she had chosen to forget, seemingly failing to remember, or acknowledge, that envy for her best friend's life and relationship was the reason for her behaviour. Looking across the room now, she saw the vivacious character that Marcus must surely have fallen in love with all those years ago. Her blonde hair had been cut into layers framing her face and deep blue eyes. The baby weight was gone and her return to work had been the steppingstone into a new identity that radiated contentment. Carrie felt a rush of shame and contrition and slowly walked out of the bar.

The air had turned to a damp drizzle and fog in the London streets such that lights appeared to float in the mist creating a strange, ethereal ambience. She found a doorway to take shelter and got her phone out and texted. "ping" ping, ping, the three texts came in simultaneously. "I'm so sorry guys but I've got a banging head I'm afraid. I've taken something for it but not working. Gonna have to miss out for once, hope you understand". C xxx ps. Love you guys and HNY smiley emoji.

The post box across the dank street beckoned to her, a prominent red pillar as if a beacon of hope drawing her ever closer. She reached into her bag and posted the letter, releasing the fear and guilt that had been buried deep inside for so long.

***

Marcus waited patiently in the suite he had booked for the night. He had pushed the boat out this time as he looked out on to the glinting lights of Park Lane's heavy traffic. The rain was beating down against the window making it hard to see detail as he tried to peer more closely, wondering why he was feeling so nervous. He glanced at his watch to check the time once again – eight o'clock finally. He had spent the last two hours alone with his thoughts as he tried to push Rachel's face out of his mind.

What a year it had been he contemplated, remembering his shock and mixed emotions over her news that she was finally pregnant. Now he had a ready-made family with two beautiful children, but along with that had come pressure; financial pressure, social pressure, sexual performance pressure, relationship pressure, peer pressure and so it went on. It hadn't left much room for anything else. But thinking, or was it fantasizing, about Carrie, helped. In fact, any escape from reality would have helped Marcus in the last twelve months.

Given the opportunity, he would have fled all responsibilities and taken off on a much delayed, gap year. Eight fifteen, and time to go down to the restaurant as agreed, don't be late she'd said, he remembered half smiling as he pictured Carrie's half jokey attempt at reprimanding him. She could talk, she was always late.

The knock on the door startled him and jolted him back to reality. He turned from the window and cautiously opened the door, heart thumping, perhaps she had changed her mind.

Rachel stood at the door holding a bottle of champagne, smiling coyly. The long black lace dress revealed a deep V and a slit in one side. Simple, elegant, and very sexy. It had the mark of Carrie, who had of course helped to choose it, along with the heels and simple accessories. "Are you going to let me in then?" she said.

Trying quickly to piece things together, he smiled and stepped back "Sure, of course," he said realising that he had been set up. Rachel walked into the room and looked around. "Wow, Marcus this is amazing! Thanks so much, I can't believe you've done this for me," she said gushing. "So, when did you find out about the surprise?" he said playing for time. "Carrie of course darling! She told me that she'd arranged a surprise for me on New Year's Eve and that's why the girls decided to meet earlier for cocktails! The funny thing is, Carrie couldn't get there in the end, poor thing, she had a migraine or something. I'll call her tomorrow you know she's out for the count when she gets one.

Marcus was at a crossroads where each path would take his life in a different direction. He knew that Carrie had made her choice but where did that leave him. One road led to married life with Rachel and his boys. The opposite road led to no Rachel and no family; another road could lead to having the boys but no Rachel. And then there was the one that also could lead to freedom; but what did that actually mean he wondered. Freedom from what, his guilt, his thoughts, his responsibilities, his endless decisions that had to be made. Even without responsibilities, he would never be free from his thoughts.

He took the glass Rachel handed to him and looked at his wife's flushed cheeks and glassy eyes. Where had the years gone? he wondered. In fact, what meaning would their lives have if they hadn't had their sons. He touched Rachel's cheek lightly as he looked into her eyes, "Rachel, I need to." She stopped him in mid-sentence and put a finger to his lips, "Shh. I don't want to know Marcus. We're in the here and now. I know we've had a difficult year but look at us now! Let's just enjoy each other and appreciate what we have."

He so wanted to tell her everything. Tell her about his failing business, his affair with Carrie, his love for Carrie, his guilt, his growing sense of responsibility and all-consuming wish to run away from everything, but also his love for Rachel, their babies, and the prospect of their future together. Did she know, he wondered, or perhaps at the very least, suspect something. One thing he knew for sure was what a mess he was in. What would Carrie tell him he wondered. Yet again she had crept into his head messing with his psyche. He buried his face in Rachel's hair thinking things through. He knew what Carrie would say, that he was a first-class dick, and of course he was, what was he thinking of.

***

Carrie was also in a hotel room, but this one was seventy miles away in the Cotswolds. She chinked

213

glasses with Ben as they bent towards each other and kissed. "Happy New Year Carrie," he whispered between kisses. "Happy New Year," she breathed, feeling a sense of optimism and lightness she hadn't felt for years.

This felt right. He felt right. Finally, after five years of guilt and loneliness she had found somebody who could be her soul mate. They heard the church bells chime twelve signalling the new year had begun. Ping, ping, ping!

The familiar text sounds came in. As if on automatic pilot she glanced across to her phone lying on the bedside table. "Leave it!" Ben's voice commanded urgently as he took his face into his hands and looked into her eyes. "I don't know why, but this feels right Carrie.

It's something I've felt from the first time I met you, this time last year. Call it fate but I can't stop thinking about you. You fill my head every day and I long to see you all the time. I've never felt like this with anyone". He said in between kisses. Thabo's approval of Carrie had melted away the uncertainty and doubt that had prevented him from letting his guard down for so long.

Unwilling to trust his own judgement, he had observed her from afar in a bar in Johannesburg, able to watch her detached, an interloper, wanting to, but not able, to join the intimacy of the conversation between the girl he loved and his best friend.

Carrie's eyes shone as a tear began to trickle down her cheek. "I need to explain something Ben," she responded guiltily and with a heavy heart. "No! I've had enough guilt and regret this past year." He said gently smiling as he wiped the tear from her eye. "But you need to know something" she persisted, not wanting any secrets between them. "Shh, I don't want to know.

We will have no secrets between us, OK? We are here, we are together, and if you agree, we can grow together as one from now on," He kissed her again and felt the relief in her demeanour as she fell into his arms. Marriage? Yes! Babies? Hopefully, secrets? Never! Career? Who cares? Carrie's heart swelled with love and optimism, ignoring the texts that continued to ping in the background.

Jenna

Jenna sat opposite her husband Jack and smiled as they clinked glasses and brought in the New Year. She sipped the champagne slowly waiting for him to tell her that he wanted a divorce, after all, why else would he suggest an intimate dinner with her on one of the iconic nights of the year. Surely, he was prepping her for the big "I don't love you anymore". She breathed deeply and tried to hold her nerve.

"It feels a bit strange having a meal together, doesn't it?" He said looking at her carefully. "Well, it does, being relatively sober," she murmured. "I think the last time we ate out was in the summer at The Hut," Jenna said, instantly regretting the remark, as she remembered that it had led to them going to bed afterwards.

"Hmm yes," he agreed with a rueful smile as he recalled an amazing afternoon with Jenna followed by a row after he had been a stupid arse and told her he had met somebody else. Six months later and he was in a very different place. He'd had his gap year of playing the field, having few responsibilities, and oh, the impromptu sex that came from seeing a woman without ties.

But it also left him feeling unfulfilled, and if push came to shove, lonely. He missed the unconditional love and friendship he had for over fifteen years with Jenna, he missed his boys, and he missed family life. But, he contemplated, he had also grown emotionally. He didn't dare say anything to Jenna who seemed to have taken on a new lease of life physically and psychologically.

He looked at the short blonde hair style, bright blue eyes, and mischievous smile that he had always loved. One word out of place and he could blow it.

She gaily gabbled on telling him one anecdote after the other about work, or the boys, or the girls' nights in. Her hands moved animatedly as she told him about her suspicion that Hattie had fallen for a woman and her concerns for Rob. Her nervousness meant that the champagne was contributing to the free talking as she topped up her glass.

He leaned forward and put the pebble from his pocket into her hand. She paused for a moment, "Oh you still have it," she said. "Well, it's not the exact one but I always carry the quiet stone when I'm with you," he said smiling. She was just about to retort her defence when he put his finger to her lips "Shh. Remember, the rule is when you hold the stone, you do not speak."

She opened her mouth to protest and then shut it silently and breathed deeply. The pebble had been a playful game between them for years when one day on a beach in Wales, he picked up a pebble and told her to not speak if she was holding the stone.

He kissed her to compensate. And of course, it was typical of Jack's humour to make fun of Jenna's spiritual, personal development interests by giving her a quiet pebble. She opened her mouth to say something again and closed it, seeing the humour but also feeling frustrated. She sat back and sipped her champagne.

"I've missed this, Jen." He said quietly looking at her and noticing the light bouncing off her blonde hair that seemed to have a glow that gave it radiance. He continued, "I've missed you. I've missed the boys," Jenna wanted to immediately retort, "well not enough to stop yourself from sharing another woman's bed," but stopped herself, still clutching the stone in the palm of her hand. Nina Simone's smooth voice resonated across the restaurant, "It's a new day. It's a new dawn. It's a new life." And then the sucker punch, "And I'm feeling good", trumpets blasting took Jenna's breath away as she put the stone on the table analysing how she felt.

She had been through a lot this year and had managed to come through the tunnel of despair and out the other side. No longer did she feel the powerless one, suddenly she was feeling empowered, strong, and resilient.

How would she feel if they put the year behind them and started again, as if nothing had happened? She looked at the handsome face opposite her, carefully taking in the natural upward curve of his mouth that always gave the impression he was not being serious.

The longer hair suited him, and the new younger outfits seemed to show a different side to the Jack she married. She still fancied him, she knew that, but would she still, if they just slotted back into married life, she wondered. Their fingers touched briefly sending an electric current through her. He was still wearing his wedding ring, she noticed.

They finished the bottle of champagne as Jack took her hand and said, "I know you might think this is a bit weird, but I wondered if you wanted to come back to mine for a bit." Just saying it felt weird, but it also sounded exciting. He wanted her to visit his place, the apartment that he had made his own, that had his stamp on it, and was his personal space.

Now he was feeling empowered. She felt a ripple of excitement run through her that ended with butterflies fluttering in her chest and then down to her stomach. Come on Jen, take a hold of yourself for God's sake she told herself. It is only Jack after all. "Yes OK," she said lightly, and then qualified the acceptance with a get out clause, "I could always get a taxi back I suppose." Jack ignored the response, standing up. "Great! Let's get a cab outside."

***

Jack turned the key in the lock and pushed the door open for Jen to walk in. Lights were already on as a warm ambient glow filled the spacious modern sitting room. He busied himself getting the drinks as she casually took in the guitar propped up in the corner and a novel left open on the side table.

His extensive CD collection and stereo took up one wall upon which modern art and black and white framed photographs formed a haphazard display that somehow worked. This didn't feel like Jack at all she contemplated. She didn't realise that he liked art and photography sufficiently enough to hang it on a wall.

"I like the photographs," she shouted through to the kitchen. "Yeh, I'm quite proud of those, my first attempt," he said, walking into the lounge with two glasses and a bottle of wine in hand. "Wow! I had no idea," she said, feeling embarrassed.

What else didn't she know she wondered? Here right under her nose, her husband had been living a different life to the one that they shared eighteen months before. She moved uncomfortably in her seat and took a sip of wine.

"What?" he said, crossing his leg casually and resting it on his knee, arm on the back of the sofa. He was so near her she could almost feel his fingers at the back of her neck. "I don't know," she said shrugging. "I suppose I had this picture of your place looking like a slightly better version of your man shed," she said, trying not to blush.

"Well, I'd like to think it is a more sophisticated version of my shed. It gives me space, I play my music, I potter about doing stuff, if that's what you mean," he said smiling. "Do you play your guitar much these days?" she said, feeling as if she was throwing a line to a new boyfriend, she was trying to make conversation with. "Yeh, sure. Do you want me to sing to you?"

Jenna blinked and adjusted her position trying not to get flustered as the champagne and wine began to take effect. "What? Eh no need for that," she remarked, trying to sound nonchalant, the thought crossing her mind that her ex had gone soft. "I've been writing poetry too," he said, moving closer. She gulped "really?" it was not Jen's style to be romanticised like this. "Jack," she said turning towards him to see his mouth twitching.

"You're winding me up, aren't you?" "Yes," he said with his face perfectly deadpan. "You're impossible!" she half shouted as she took a cushion from behind her back to hit him in exasperation. Jack was laughing out loud by now, the full force of the cushion hit his arm. "Sorry, I couldn't help it. I know how much you would hate being serenaded let alone the poetry reading," he responded, taking the cushion that she still had in her hands and putting it behind him. Suddenly they were face to face, just inches away so that he could feel her breathing. Here was his chance to take her face in his hands and kiss her as he had imagined for months. But he lost his nerve.

Jenna seemed so strong, beautiful, and how could he put it? She didn't seem to need him anymore, but this made him want her even more. The thought crossed his mind in a flash but before he processed the sentiment, she moved away, and the moment passed. Her cheeks were flushed, and a pink glow made its way down her slim neck.

Jenna couldn't believe how nervous she felt. Unsettled, she stood up careful not to wobble. "Can I put the kettle on?" she asked not waiting for an answer as she headed to the kitchen. Jack pushed his hair back with his hands smiling ruefully. This really was weirder than he had imagined. How could two people who had shared their lives for more than fifteen years, and brought up two sons together, feel so estranged? He wondered. But the funny thing was, that as unsettling as it was, it also felt new, exciting, and risky. He wanted her back, really wanted her back, but one wrong move and it could go tits up.

Jenna came back into the room holding a mug of coffee in each hand. Her top had moved slightly so that a bare shoulder was exposed. Jack wanted to know what bra she was wearing, or was she wearing a bra he wondered. Of course, she was she always wore a bra, and if he could remember rightly, it would be an industrial strength hold everything in bra.

She sat back down and pushed a mug towards him. "Here, I think we could both do with this.". Jenna felt Jack's presence like she had never before. His tall, athletic frame sat close by her, and she found herself willing him to touch her. They were so close, and she had blown it as usual by moving, breaking the atmosphere.

"I'm sorry Jack," she said into her coffee. "I'm so sorry that I drove you away". "Hey, you didn't do that.

It's been a hard year for both of us, but we can put it behind us, can't we?" he said, moving closer as he began to stroke the back of her neck. Feeling his fingers gently touching her, she closed her eyes taking in the moment.

Is this what it takes to mend a relationship she considered. Eighteen months hard labour including restorative justice where both parties come together to appreciate the hurt, they had caused. Because Jack had hurt Jenna. Finding out that he had slept with his female boss had hurt her big time. He hadn't said anything about her, but she knew that he'd had feelings for her at some point. What if she'd thrown him out and she was on the rebound? Jenna stiffened at the thought.

"So, what happened with your colleague?" she couldn't stop herself as the words tumbled out of her mouth. Here it was. The question hit Jack hard in his chest. He knew it was coming but hadn't anticipated the left hook that caught him unawares. If there was one way of changing an atmosphere this would be it and Jenna was good at that.

He sat up and put his head in his hands trying to find the right words. "Jen, I can't explain it and I can't excuse my behaviour. I know I've hurt you and I wish I it had never happened. I'm a total dick and it was my stupid ego that took me to a place that I should never have gone to."
"It's over then is it?" she persisted.

"It had never really begun," he said gently. There was no way he was going to tell her that he had begun to have feelings for Sarah, the sex was phenomenal, and he had rediscovered who he was through her. But he also knew that it would never last, that in time they would annoy each other and that most of all, she wasn't someone that he wanted to spend the rest of his life with.

"I want you, Jen. I want us." He said, moving nearer. "You can't remove a life-long connection from a relationship like ours."

The sun was beginning to rise when they finally fell asleep on the sofa with Jenna's head resting peacefully on Jack's shoulder. It was four hours later when Jenna heard the shower, that she peeled off her clothes and quietly joined him to wash away the past eighteen months in a morning of reignited passion.

Hattie

Hattie quietly opened the front door and tip-toed inside. It was nine thirty and whilst most festivities hadn't even started, hers were almost finished. She left the cocktail bar when the friends departed and made her way home knowing that Rob would be waiting for her. Without any plans in place for the first time in years, she walked in cautiously to the quiet atmosphere. The gleaming kitchen was offset by the flickering candlelight which had cast dancing shadows across the table laid for two. Rob sat quietly sipping a glass of red wine. "Hello."

"Hello. Where are the girls?" she said, smiling at the trouble he had gone to. "I've managed to get them both off upstairs would you believe!"

"Wow! That's amazing, thank you." The awkwardness shifting slightly as she sat down opposite him. Hattie took the glass offered to her and chinked glasses with her husband. She knew how much he loved her and that her life now was with him and their beautiful girls.

Rob looked at his wife appreciating the mane of red hair that had beguiled him from the first time he saw her dancing at that party so long ago. He wasn't sure what kind of personal journey Hattie had gone on this past year, but he recognised it has taken her along a path of self-discovery.

Now, the woman sitting opposite him, was the woman he had fallen in love with, all those years ago as a student. The wildness and unpredictability had come back. The quirky dress sense had returned.

The spontaneity was resumed, such that as frustrating as it was, his disorganised, slightly chaotic wife would announce that she had plans over a weekend and would take herself off to a gallery opening.

There would always be a side to her that Rob would never be part of, he knew that. For ten years she had adopted the role of dutiful wife and mother but somehow, she seemed lost. Now this past year she appeared to have risen from the ashes like a phoenix from a fire and he knew that her spirit, once unleashed, was likely to gather momentum.

He watched her throwing back her head laughing as she retold some of the stories shared with the girls that evening, drawn to her enigmatic charm and extrovert nature that was the opposite of him. This felt good. It felt right.

The old Hattie was back and one that he knew could not be controlled and who by her very nature would follow the path of least resistance. He had her, they had their girls, and they were happy. The clock struck midnight and they chinked glasses as a text pinged its way to Hattie's phone.

"Happy New Year, babe. I miss you. I want you. I need you. We should be together. xxx"

Hattie quickly responded without hesitation, turning away as she texted.

"HNY my love. Mon chere, je taime, je t'adore. Let's make a pact to NEVER spend NYE apart again my darling. I miss you. I need you. I want to feel you. You've opened my world. I won't forget. We will find a way. Our secret, I promise. Next year xxxx."

'Who was that?' Rob asked casually, trying to hide his irritation.

'Only the girls, you know what they're like,' she replied on automatic pilot as unwittingly, the baton of secrecy had been passed to a new team member.

Chapter 21

There's a thin line between love and hate. Being in love is obsessive. We cannot stop thinking, dreaming, wishing, and wanting to be together. Could it be, that hate is the same in disguise?

<u>Marcus</u>

Marcus put on his jacket and strapped the boys into the buggy ready to head out of the front door to the shops. Rachel was managing the gallery and not due back until early evening as the demands of her new job had begun to seep into their lives. He didn't mind though. It gave the time and space for him to pursue new interests or rather a "new take" on old interests as he turned the handle and kicked the door open with his foot and manoeuvred the buggy out of the narrow doorway.

His car sat in the drive flirting for his attention. He had barely closed the door behind him when he turned tail and opened the door again with an urgency as he quickly found the car keys and adjusted the seats to accommodate his sons.

He glanced at his watch – 9am, early for a Saturday but not early for Carrie's regular morning run in Battersea Park. If he could get there by 9.30am he might just catch her, his mind racing as he pulled out of the drive, he cautiously looked around to check if any neighbours were out and about.

He loved these outings he contemplated as the traffic lights turned red on the approach and the car slowly grew to a halt. He glanced in the rear-view mirror and smiled at the sleeping faces, contentedly turned towards each other. A swell of love entered his chest as he pulled away smiling, excited for the day ahead.

He always felt excited when he saw Carrie, although these days, seeing her was becoming increasingly difficult as she seemed more elusive, Rachel was more demanding, and of course the troubles and stresses of his business demanded his attention more than he would like. Never mind he thought as he parked near the entrance to the park, grateful that Battersea residents didn't seem to be weekend early risers.

Today was designated for him and Carrie, and the twins of course he thought as he carefully put the babies into the buggy and strapped them in.

He walked to his usual spot and sat down on the park bench under a shady tree. The spring sunshine had begun to filter through its leaves, leaving a dappled light and the promise of a beautiful, unusually warm day. It was Easter weekend and there was an excitement in the air that comes with a long public holiday weekend, good weather and the unfurling optimism that Spring brings, confirming that Winter has finally ended. He glanced at his watch – 10am. Hopefully he wasn't too late.

The park had begun to wake up as dog walkers, strollers, joggers and serious runners had each begun their usual routes, nodding in acknowledgement as they passed each other. Marcus was fascinated by the body language, what they were wearing, and body type. Fat men, fat women, or perhaps overweight was a more polite term he thought.

Then there were the gym freaks, perfectly toned, muscle vests, sweat dripping off them, and of course the dog walkers. They were a funny bunch – and it was true, they did look like their dogs! And then of course there was Carrie, darling, unique, irreplaceable Carrie. Unlike any of the other categories, she could not be placed in a box he thought.

He looked into the distance and spotted her running with headphones plugged in. I wonder what she's listening to he thought. He leaned forward, elbows on his knees and put the binoculars to his eyes for a better look. Her shiny chestnut ponytail bounced enticingly as she picked up pace with a look of concentration on her face.

She was wearing the fluorescent orange vest she wore to the gym and black leggings – he loved those as they really showed off her figure, which he of course knew intimately. It was just frustrating that he had not been able to explore it again he thought, since Ben had muscled his way into her life. The thought irritated him as he took out his phone and captured her running.

He knew the letter she had sent was a phase and he would just have to be patient, after all, New Year's Eve was a few months away; she was bound to come to her senses by then. She seemingly was making her way towards him, but appeared oblivious to everything, except meeting her time target.

He looked down and adjusted the babies" blanket casually until she had run past. That was it, the brief interlude of lust and love diminished as she casually ran past him as if he were a stranger, a faceless being who had no connection, no past, or no future with her.

Carrie slowed down and walked the last ten minutes as part of her usual cool down. She wasn't sure why, but she felt slightly on edge as the muscles in her neck and shoulder became tense. She moved her head slowly from side to side, rounding her shoulders to loosen up, trying to not think about the uneasy feeling she had had over the past few weeks. Was she being paranoid, or just overly emotional due to the pressure of work, she wondered?

Her relationship with Ben was deepening. Yes, she could finally regard it as a relationship, something that was committed, mutually exclusive, loving and forward looking. But recent events had begun to disturb her which she had not shared with him. There was nothing in particular, she considered, as she approached her tree-lined road, just a few odd unexplained mishaps here and there.

Small things had gone missing from the apartment. Nothing of great significance but items that somehow, she seemed to have misplaced and not been able to find. There was the silk scarf that she had bought in Portobello Market one Saturday afternoon whilst enjoying the bustle and bohemian atmosphere of one of her favourite parts of London.

She had only worn it once and was certain that it had been hanging in the hallway with other accessories, but it had disappeared in the last month and was nowhere to be seen. Her underwear drawer looked different. Now that was being paranoid, she reprimanded herself internally. Who on earth is so pedantic that their underwear drawer is ordered in a particular way that they would notice any changes?

She let herself in and made her way up to the shower, damp with exhaustion. As the pounding water hit her skin she relaxed and closed her eyes, unaware of the persistent knocking on the front door. Hearing something in the background, she quickly dried herself and cautiously peeped through the security hole wondering who was visiting so early in the morning.

Marcus beamed at her holding a bag of croissants. Cass, I was just passing with the boys and thought I'd see on the off chance if you fancied sharing breakfast? She opened the door wearily as she didn't want a confrontation on the doorstep. "What are you doing here Marcus? How can you be just passing? You live on the other side of town, for God's sake!"

He walked in ignoring her, handing one of the babies over. "You're a natural with them Cass," he said, walking into the kitchen with the other baby on his shoulder oblivious to her discontent.

She found a rug from the sofa and carefully put the baby down, watching him covertly. He was in a world of his own and seemed preoccupied. His dress sense had altered so that he no longer wore the trademark chinos and designer shirts but had adopted a grungy scruffy look.

The stubble on his face had morphed into an unkempt beard, his jeans had seen better days, and his t-shirt appeared to have been taken from the laundry bin without a second thought. His face was lined and showed signs of stress.

"How are you then?" she said with a deliberate air of nonchalance. "Yeh good," he said lying. "I just wanted to see you that's all. We never seem to see each other these days" he said sipping his coffee. "That's because we are in separate relationships Marcus.

Things are different now, you know that." She picked up the baby and walked towards him gesturing to the door. "You have to go now, Marcus. I'm going out."

He followed her into the hall as she strapped the baby into the buggy, standing aside for him to do the same. "Thanks for the croissants," she said, opening the door. "It was a lovely gesture but next time, do it for Rachel, she'd love that." His demeanour changed as he smiled tight lipped pushing the buggy out of the door. "Yeh, it was nice seeing you Cass. Eh, until next time then," he said over his shoulder. Carrie closed the door, disturbed, something wasn't right. It was three weeks later when she found her instincts were correct.

Marcus

In the past three months, Marcus had taken on a different persona. It hadn't been deliberate, but had rather evolved over time he considered, as he sipped the cold beer he had just taken from the fridge. He lay across the

232

sofa as the mid-day sun filtered across his face and closed his eyes.

The bottle stood upright in his hands which rested gently on his stomach as he breathed slowly, feeling the gentle rise and ebb. He quite liked this new look. One where he didn't always have to have an ironed shirt for work, didn't have to wear smart trousers, didn't even have to shave! It felt liberating.

He had ceased caring about what other people thought about him and was choosing to live his life the way he wanted, except it wasn't quite what he wanted because Carrie wasn't part of it anymore. For the past five years she had been his, if only for one night but the sweetness and intimacy they had kept him going until the following year.

Things had changed since she had been with Ben, but he was convinced that it was a mere passing fling and if he waited, she would return to his arms. In the meantime, he was prepared to just see her casually when he could, just as mates he thought, sipping the beer. He turned his attention to last New Year's Eve trying to recall what they had done, and then remembered that Rachel had intercepted the evening. Yes, that's right, he was supposed to be with Cass, but she had set it up for Rachel to go instead. He tried to recall the evening but could not remember much about the detail, was it really that insignificant? He always remembered every detail of the nights he'd had with Cass.

Feeling aroused, he put the beer down and walked into the quiet kitchen. The boys must be having their nap he thought as he quietly walked upstairs to check on them.

The nursery curtains were half closed as they lay sleeping gently on their backs with their hands above their heads as only babies do. Feeling a rush of love, he closed the door and walked to the master bedroom looking for Rachel.

She was bending over making the bed and half turned as he walked in and stood behind her, pulling her towards him. Shocked and slightly embarrassed she allowed him to caress her before turning towards him. "Mmm, what's brought this on?" she said as he kissed her neck. "Nothing, I just want to be with you." He said as he put his hands through her hair. "Marcus, the boys..." she said whispering.

"Shh, they're fast asleep, I've just checked on them," he said, undoing her top. They fell on to the bed as he continued to release his pent-up emotions kissing her passionately and whispering her name into her ear. Except Rachel did not hear her name, but the name of one of her best friends.

Chapter 22

Rachel

A constant cloud of anxiety hovered over Rachel and rested on her shoulders like a lead weight. She eased herself from the floor where she had been sorting through a pile of washing and stood up to release the tension in her neck.

Sick with fear, she could not help, but to continue reliving the moment, that she had heard Carrie's name instead of hers. Was she being paranoid she agonized, as she moved her neck from side to side?

"What did you say?" she asked pushing him away. "Nothing, what are you going on about?" he said kissing her neck and mouth.

She should have pushed him off her there and then, she recalled. Instead, she allowed him to continue as she closed her eyes waiting for it to be over. "Do you love me, Marcus?" she said, watching him pull his t-shirt over his head after.

"Of course, I love you," he replied without hesitation. His bed head hair and stubble made him look even more handsome she thought. Surely if he was having an affair, he would be making more effort, not going the other way, she tried convincing herself.

He bent towards her and kissed her gently. "Come on, the boys will be rousing," he said, smiling as he opened the door quietly. This new persona disturbed Rachel as she reflected on the change in appearance and attitude towards his work and business. It was unheard of for him to not go and check on progress of a development project for a few hours at the weekend.

She got dressed and crept downstairs, curious to see him from a distance as if an on-looker peering through a neighbour's window. She quietly opened the kitchen door that was ajar, and peered round to see him indulging in another beer, while the babies sat playing with their toys on a mat on the floor. He was engrossed in his phone unaware of her presence. It was two hours later when Marcus had gone to football that she decided to take back control and end the uncertainty she had been feeling for months.

The indelible imprint of people's lives is impossible to erase through the inter-connectedness of social media. Somewhere, somehow, Rachel was determined to uncover what was going on in her husband's life, that she was not part of. It felt wrong to look at his emails and Facebook, but still she found herself scrolling down the history and string of conversations, but to no avail. Mundane communication between contractors and builders, estate agents and football club arrangements. She continued past the junk and relevant hoping for an answer but found nothing.

Disconcertedness and relief fought for attention as she battled with incredulity that she had found nothing, but nevertheless continued to feel that something was not right.

"Secrets are my currency: I deal with them for a living. The secrets of desire, of what people really want, and of what they fear the most. The secrets of why love is difficult, sex complicated, living painful and death so close and placed far away. Why are pleasure and punishment closely related?" ("Something to Tell You" – Hanif Kureishi)

Rachel put the book down and considered the opening lines. It was true, pleasure and punishment could be closely related she contemplated. One thing that she had decided for sure was to find out what was going on in Marcus's head.

Her parents had always felt that he wasn't good enough for her, why, she was not sure. Their relationship had been such a whirlwind at the beginning, and she knew that she had been swept away with his charm and good looks.

The seamless transition from casual date to lifelong partner, seemed to have missed the few vital steps of getting to know and understand each other, to know what drives them, what is important and not important, and what secrets, if any, did they hold. Just like the words in the book, secrets of love and secrets of what they feared the most. Did Marcus love her, she wondered, and why had she always felt that his heart was given to someone else, but who?

She texted Carrie. "Hi Cass, what are you up to? Don't suppose you fancy a drink this evening. Got a sitter so can go out for once!" Signing off with a hand praying emoji.

Carrie considered the invitation uncertain how she felt. It had been a while since she had seen Rachel on her own and the recent behaviour of Marcus was of concern. She wanted to distance herself from him completely, but equally she felt it her duty to give her friend the emotional support she needed.

She wavered between guilt and obligation as her moral compass moved between the two feelings that weighed heavily in her heart. "Yeh, why not?" she texted back thinking, she owed it to her friend even though it was the last thing she wanted to do.

They met in their usual haunt, the cosy pub at the corner of Rachel's Road so that she would be on hand if the sitter needed her, Marcus was out playing football and as it usually followed an evening in the club bar, they both knew that they had the whole evening together to put the world to right.

Rachel was already sitting in the corner nursing a glass of merlot when Carrie walked in, looking around. A few regulars propped up the bar chatting and exchanging comments with the bar staff, a group of young women were laughing together over a bottle of wine, and an older couple sat opposite each other with the silence of familiarity that doesn't require conversation, but just the presence of being together.

Needing Dutch courage, she waved to Rachel and pointed to the bar before heading over to get a bottle of wine. No need to stick to a glass she thought as she'd come by Uber and could easily drop Rachel off on her way back.

"So, lovely to see you. How have you been?" she said throwing her jacket on to the chair beside her and pecking her cheek. "I'm fine, the babies are fine, I'm not so sure about Marcus though," Rachel said, launching straight in, and much earlier than she had planned. Carrie sipped the wine playing for time, while she considered her response. "Oh, what makes you say that?"

"Have you seen him lately?" Carrie's heart beated faster until she realised it was a rhetorical question as Rachel continued, "He's changed Cass, I don't know if he's depressed and not telling me, or if something else is going on, but he's dishevelled; he doesn't take any care about his appearance. He drinks beer during the day which he never used to do, and he just seems preoccupied the whole time."

The guilt seeped deep into her core as Carrie put the glass down, looking down at the table. "He might be depressed; it is a possibility?" she said looking up. The thought hadn't entered Rachel's head as a reason for his behaviour, realising then that her earlier reference to depression had been a throw away comment, said without any real thought or empathy behind it.

She was aware how self-centred she could be, considering that this could be a possibility. Carrie felt unusually uncomfortable and wanted to run away from the pub as far as she could. Here she was, facing her best friend who was talking about her husband taking on a new persona and behaviour, and asking *her*, Carrie for advice. This was not good. It felt wrong. She needed to make an excuse and get away as soon as she was able.

She began to fumble in her handbag searching for her phone.

"Rachel, I'm so sorry but I have to go," she said in desperation, unable to make it sound casual. "What? Already? We haven't even got started yet!" Rachel protested.

She ignored Carrie's request to leave and continued "So have you seen him then?" she persisted lightly. Carrie hesitated for a moment, "No, of course not, why would I? I'm working 24/7 most of the time, and in between, I rarely have time for anything, other than Ben and seeing you, and the rest of the gang, you know that." She responded heatedly, trying not to sound defensive.

"I just wondered that's all. It's just that Marcus mentioned he'd dropped by?" Rachel replied, trying to hold herself together.

"Really?" Carrie could not understand why Marcus would have told Rachel, and what his intention might be, by doing so. She hesitated. "Well, yes he did pass by on Saturday morning, but he was only around for about 15 minutes as I had to go out. I didn't speak to him for long, and not sure why he even came round, to be honest."

She shifted uncomfortably in her seat hoping that Rachel hadn't noticed the rush of colour that had made its way from her neck to her cheeks. She forced a smile to soften the contradiction. "How are things between you now?" I got the impression that your relationship was back on an even keel, and he was loving being a daddy?"

"He adores the boys," Rachel acknowledged. "But something's wrong, I just can't put my finger on it" she shrugged. Carrie felt compelled to say something even though she didn't want to. "What do you think is going on then?"

"I really don't know, but I'm definitely going to find out" Rachel shrugged taking a large sip from her glass. The need to take any suspicion as far away from herself as possible was a survival tactic for Carrie, survival of her friendship, survival of her relationship with Ben, survival of her own integrity.

"You know that I'd do anything for you Rachel don't you? Ben and I are thinking of moving to South Africa you know. I've been meaning to say for ages, but I really think he's the one. Who knows, I might be able to have a family like you one day. Don't let this spoil what you have hun. You tried for a family for so long and by the miracle of life you've been blessed." She said squeezing her friend's hand.

Rachel thought back to the lines in the book that they were reading, privately thinking that secrets were also the currency from which Carrie made a living. "Come on let's go," she said, glancing down at the empty bottle of wine smiling. "You're probably right".

* * *

It was a rare weekend that Rachel and the boys were to stay for the weekend at her parents. She was looking forward to a different environment where she would be spoilt and comforted by mum and dad, and for the first time in weeks, had a feeling of optimism and excitement. She busied herself in the bedroom sorting through clothes, pulling out jackets and tops haphazardly and throwing them on to the crisp white bed linen that was her hallmark.

It wasn't until she noticed Marcus's tailored jackets hanging discreetly at the back that she momentarily stopped and remembered his old style. It had been so long since he last dressed like that, she had almost forgotten how much he had changed. She touched the soft wool jacket lightly and ran her fingers along the line of the revered collar. Why on earth had he stopped wearing this, she wondered, taking the jacket out to look at it. Pure wool, single breasted in a French navy, with a dark blue silk lining. It exuded style and quality and had been Marcus's signature wardrobe when he was on form, nothing like the unkept grungy look that he had adopted these past few months.

Almost instinctively she put her hand in the inside pocket. Her fingers touched something; the crisp folds of thick white paper, carefully folded, hidden, deliberate, secretive. Yet more secrets, more currency to trade with.

Amidst the pile of clothes, she sat down and carefully opened the folded paper. The printed invoice, an opaque malediction that revealed a printout for a room booking payment for the penthouse suite of a hotel in Chelsea harbour. The date was more than a year ago on New Year's Eve. Her heart sank trying to process the date and recall how and where she had spent the day.

Gradually the dawn of realisation came to her, as she remembered that Marcus had always "worked" on New Year's Eve for years, maintaining that he was doing his accounts to meet the annual tax deadline in January.

Could that be true? She examined the invoice closely which showed an early check out at 5pm, still enough time to return home for the evening festivities. She could hear the beating of her heart in the quietness of the morning. He had an office, so no need to rent a room. Maybe he took a prostitute she considered as her brain began to filter all the possibilities.

That would be the most likely scenario she reasoned, as a rage of anger and betrayal seeped its way deep inside. As if she had been punched violently in the stomach, Rachel felt a wave of nausea and bile in her throat. She ran to the bathroom and threw up in the toilet knowing in her gut that this would not have been the only time.

Momentary peace came later that evening as the fire glowed in her family home and she sipped wine in the safe familiarity of her parent's lounge. The boys were sound asleep upstairs as she carefully recounted her fears to her parents who sat listening quietly.

Prostitute, Carrie, work colleague, each possibility was discussed at length and weighed against probability, the least likely being Carrie, after all, she was Rachel's best friend and was in a strong stable relationship. It was unthinkable to even put her name in the mix. But of course, Rachel had deliberately left out certain details to her parents such as the whispering of Carrie's name when they had sex, the odd, slightly incoherent sleep talk, that she heard occasionally, and of course, the long-term flirtatious friendship they had enjoyed from the first time they had met.

As much as she had tried to ignore the signs, the thought continued to eat away at her, making her question and recall every moment that Carrie had been over to visit. Book group meetings, could she have met Marcus before she arrived, she wondered, it was a possibility.

They talked until there was nothing left inside her. Rachel had nothing else to give and nothing else to take from the situation. Finally, after months of suspicion and uncertainty, she now knew that he had been seeing someone.

What was unclear, was if it was the same person, or a different person each time. In many ways, she would have preferred the latter as at least it might indicate that it was just sex, nothing more.

However, an emotional tie with somebody cuts deep into an already wounded heart and she also knew that there was a point of no return whatever reality presented itself. She cried herself asleep, exhausted.

Chapter 23

"Tired of lying in the sunshine, staying home to watch the rain. You are young and life is long and there is time to kill today. And then one day you find ten years have got behind you. No one then one day told you when to run, you missed the starting gun" lyrics Pink Floyd "Time" Dark Side of the Moon

It was Sunday evening and Marcus was indulging himself content in his own company as the rich sounds from the stereo filled the room. His eyes were closed as he lay along the sofa with his hands resting behind his head. Rachel closed the door quietly and put her bag down as he became aware of her presence and opened his eyes. He smiled with genuine affection, "Hi, where are the boys?" he said sitting up. "I've left them with mum and dad for a couple of days. They've missed them and said they would be happy to have them to give me a break."

She looked at him closely hoping for a sign but couldn't read his face. If anything, he seemed more relaxed, he had even had a shave and haircut. He walked over and bent down to kiss her.

"So, that means we should make hay while the sun shines so to speak," he said softly into her hair. Rachel closed her eyes and breathed deeply; it wasn't going to be easy. Was this the start of a new beginning, or the beginning of the end she wondered as the words played back in her head, "And then one day you find ten years have got behind you. No one told you when to run, you missed the starting gun".

Chapter 24

Daffodils had pushed their way through the bare flowerbeds in the garden and had formed a quiet carpet of yellow and green and a visual hint that Spring had made its mark. Rachel drew back the curtains and peered through the window to the garden. It was a breezy day in May as the weak sun continued to fight against the backdrop of cloud, finally resting to illuminate the flowers.

She sipped her coffee and recalled the discussion she'd had with Hattie and Jenna the evening before and the look of confusion, followed by incredulity and then horror. "No way!" said Jenna. "You are joking," said Hattie, after they agreed together that she was becoming paranoid and bordering on obsessive.

The truth was that she had become obsessed with trying to discover who she had married because she believed that Marcus had been living a double life. Most of her time, when she was not working in the gallery, was spent looking through his emails, sifting through paperwork, and emptying out pockets of his jeans and trousers. She had no evidence that Carrie was involved other than the whisper of her name three months before when he was on top of her during a moment of passion.

She recalled the time she had told Jenna that she thought Marcus had said Carrie's name when he was asleep but of course she had only heard a mumble of something that sounded like it. Hattie felt disloyal and uncomfortable as the conversation once again turned to Rachel's conviction that Marcus was having an affair

247

with their best friend. The guilt behind her own infidelity grappled with her conscience whilst she quietly pushed Francoise to the back of her mind. She tried to reason with herself as she stood in the queue to order a second round of coffee, grateful for the space to process her own thoughts, as well as not having to discuss the situation further.

Her and Rob had an unspoken agreement that whatever Hattie got up to when she went away for weekends in Cambridge, or anywhere else, were not discussed in detail. Hattie would gladly volunteer that she was having a girly weekend away, but Rob chose never to put pressure on her to spend more time with him or question why she was spending so much time with Francoise, it wasn't ideal, but somehow it worked. She decided that she shouldn't compare her situation, but equally she could not voice an opinion on Marcus whatever was going on.

By the time she returned to the table, Jenna had moved the subject on, and Rachel seemed content to let go of the need to dissect and deconstruct every detail and conversation that she had had with Marcus or Carrie. Secretly Rachel knew she was alone in her quest for justice. She just had to find a way to show everybody she was right, and the moment came just a few weeks later.

***

Rachel lay in the bath and closed her eyes, basking in the warmth of the water and natural oils. The solitary silence of the empty house invited introspection. Its quiet walls, holding secrets that were not shared. Secrets that both she and Marcus held. Secrets of past owners and secrets of the future.

The unfinished business of Marcus's secret continued to dominate all thoughts. "Failing to plan, is planning to fail," she thought. Yes! she needed a plan but what? At this point in time, she had nothing other than a gut instinct and an old receipt from a hotel. What happened last year, she tried to recall, closing her eyes. She replayed the scene in her mind trying to remember the details of the evening but the memory that came to mind was not of her night with Marcus, but the texts she had got from Carrie and the furtive meeting they'd had in the café on the high street.

She'd forgotten about the excitement she felt when Carrie's text came through three days before New Year's Eve. If she hadn't been having lunch with Jen, she might have dismissed the idea as pure fantasy, the idea of a romantic night in a hotel with her husband who had grown to be more of a stranger then partner over the 12 months before, seemed incongruous, but it was Carrie's Christmas present to them so how could she refuse?

Jenna and Rachel had just emptied the last drop of wine from the bottle into their glasses and were enjoying the warm fuzzy glow of a long lunch, loosened tongues, and old friends, putting the world to right. The anecdote that Jenna shared with Rachel about her first day back in the city sparked raucous laughter that made Rachel cry as she wiped away the sniggers and giggles of shared in-jokes between them. Ping! The phone on the table sounded and lit up to show a text coming through. Jenna looked at Rachel and winked, "Go on, it's probably Marcus sexting you."

"Ha! No it's my other bloke on the side," she said, casually opening the phone. "That's weird, it's Cass actually". She handed the phone to Jenna who read the text out loud, "Hi hon, I didn't tell you at Christmas as I wanted to make it a surprise but I've booked a room for you and Marcus on NYE so you can have some time together. He thinks it's just dinner so don't say anything to him. Spk soon xxx."

"Wow, that's amazing and typical Cass," Jenna said smiling and shaking her head in disbelief. "How come she hasn't done anything like that for any of us?" she said jokingly. "Well perhaps if you went off the rails and had stolen half the contents of Mothercare, she might," said Rachel. "I've been a basket case this past year. Honestly, I don't know if I'd have come through it without you guys," Rachel said shrugging.

The bath water had become cold as the memory stung Rachel in the pit of her stomach. She got out of the bath troubled, as more recollections began to compete for attention. They went shopping the next day she remembered. It was Carrie's idea as she said she had some time off between Christmas and New Year. The pouring rain had dampened their spirits slightly as they compensated for it over a cappuccino before deciding which shops to visit. "Really Cass I'm not that bothered to be honest," Rachel said smiling, "I've got loads of stuff in my wardrobe that I haven't worn for years."

"My point exactly!" said Carrie. "Come on, you need a new wardrobe and at the very least, something for New Year's Eve". Rachel had never recalled Carrie so animated and excited, especially over shopping with her. Thinking back, in the twenty years of friendship, she couldn't recall if they had ever been clothes shopping together. Their taste was so different for a start – Rachel very Boden and M&S, and Carrie more FCUK and designer. It wasn't reluctance she recalled, but more caution, she felt as they entered an independent boutique. Carrie pulled out a black halter neck maxi made from silk. "Wow, Rachel this would look fab on you!" she exclaimed, putting it against her. "Oh, I'm not sure Cass, it's a bit revealing, isn't it? Also, don't you think it will show all my bumps and lumps?"

An hour and several outfits later, Carrie stood at the counter flashing a gold credit card, insisting that she was paying for the dress.

Rachel was in awe of this confident, sassy, fun-loving friend who had the ability to persuade anybody to not only change their mind about something, but to also be completely happy about the decision. By the time they had left the shop, Rachel was excited, feeling sexy and could not wait to turn into the seductress that Carrie had painted.

The detail did not stop there Rachel remembered. The appointment at the hairdressers was unexpected but welcomed. They went into a top salon in Bond Street and spent the rest of the afternoon being pampered which included a complete make over for Rachel, again paid for by Carrie. By this time, she had stopped even expecting to pay for anything that day, she had stopped feeling guilty and had begun to enjoy the self-indulgence, believing that she deserved it.

She looked around the trendy salon, sipping prosecco and closed her eyes enjoying the moment. Her peripheral vision caught Carrie laughing with the hair stylist cutting her hair. This is the life she thought. This is how Carrie lives her life on a daily basis; she could not help but feel a twinge of envy despite her friend's unconditional generosity. Now looking back, envy had turned into simmering anger as she weighed up the possibility that the present from Carrie was her way of alleviating the guilt of betrayal.

She rifled through Marcus's jackets trying to remember what he might have worn that evening. Twelve months previously, remembering details such as clothes were hazy, but then again, New Year's Eve is not like any other day of the year. Thought's racing, her need to find the suit Marcus wore that evening led her to frantically search through trouser and jacket pockets.

Frustrated and on the brink of tears she sank on to the bed and put her head in her hands. Was she being completely unreasonable, looking for answers to questions that need not exist in the first place? The mental strain hovered over her like a grey cloud that was ever omnipresent. Fearful of her mental capacity to handle the stress, and a downward decline to old habits, her creative mind fuelled graphic images of a story unfolding as she slept night after night.

Now it was Rachel who tossed and turned, sleeping fitfully, as Marcus lay peacefully unaware beside his wife.

***

"You know when you've had a dream and it's so vivid that you wake up and believe it's really happened?" Rachel said to Jenna as they sat in the busy café on the local high street. Jenna stirred her coffee and nodded with a feeling that more was to come.

She felt uncomfortable at this continued diatribe that had taken over all other conversation with Rachel. "Go on," she said quietly. "I literally woke up in the middle of the night and had this feeling that Marcus had left me. It was so real that I had to look to see if he was in bed with me." Rachel explained animatedly. "And I guess he was lying next to you, wasn't he?" Jenna said in quiet exasperation. "Yes, he was.

But I realised that he had actually left me a long time ago. He may be with me physically Jen, but he's not been with me emotionally for years. In the dream I literally saw him with Carrie, they were in a hotel room and then I woke up."

The feeling stayed with her all day. An uncomfortable, hollow emptiness that was fuelled by fear and anxiety as reality reared its head in the form of a mobile phone. Serendipity took Rachel to find a battery for the TV remote and rummage through Marcus's man box as she jokingly called it. The rusty and battered sweet tin from the fifties found in a boot sale housed everything from old coins and badges to batteries and string. It contained a collection of cigarette cards that he had always maintained were valuable, USB sticks and a series of random keys which opened doors to long forgotten histories.

The mobile lay amongst the accumulated debris without any hint of covert deception, innocently lying on top, waiting to be discovered. Rachel took the phone and plugged it into the socket to charge, hovering over it with anticipation. Unable to wait, the green light came on as she opened the phone with trembling hands. Password locked, she grappled with possibilities, trying Marcus's date of birth. For once his lack of imagination paid off as the apps sprang to life and she opened the text messages.

The stream of dialogue felt like a punch in the stomach as Rachel flopped down on the sofa and became party to a conversation she had never been invited to join. She flicked open the photos and scrolled through hundreds of pictures of Carrie, mostly alone, some close-up and some from a distance. The montage of scenes pieced together a story that had remained unread for years, how many exactly she wasn't sure, but the truth stared her in the face. She put the phone back hastily to cover her tracks. She needed time to think.

***

Rachel

I sit down on the worn armchair covered with rugs to hide the patches on the arms and back. It was a remnant from the days when we had no money and bought furniture second-hand. Somehow it has followed us from house to house. A bitter-sweet reminder of our journey through life and relationship. The first time we saw it at the back of a junk shop in The Lanes. The excitement and challenge of carrying it through Brighton's narrow streets to our tiny one-bedroom flat at the top of a Turkish coffee shop. Manoeuvring it up the narrow stairs and squeezing it through the doorway exhausted and drained with sweat, we fall on top of it laughing, me sitting on Marcus's lap kissing him on the lips.

After, it took pride of place in the lounge. Our first piece of furniture; sat prominently under the recessed Georgian arched window so that we could read easily with natural light. It wasn't so worn then I recall. The dark pink upholstery with blue piping was unusual for the style and age – another point of discussion, consideration, elaboration, compromise. "I'm sorry but it's pink!" Marcus said in exasperation. "I don't do pink", he said emphatically. "It's not pink," I responded. "Think of it as dark rose. It's typical of Victorian colours." Of course, he conceded. He always conceded then. He loved me, and *only me* then.

We joked how the chair would be an heirloom passed on to the kids we didn't yet have. Little did we know what the future had in store for us. Now it sits demoted alone in the corner of the study we never use. My feeble attempt to maintain its status was to throw bright kilim cushions against the back with contrasting blankets on the arm. Haphazard and incongruent like our marriage, some things "worked", others didn't quite fit.

My shaking hand, holding the phone feels clammy. I rest it on my lap and try his birth date as a possible password. Sometimes knowing someone as well as you know yourself can be a blessing, as much as a curse, I consider. The phone springs to life. No screen saver I note. I touch the photos icon and there it is – proof that I am looking for but hoping not to find. Photos of Carrie. Her smiling face masks the deceit and betrayal of a twenty-year friendship. I continue to swipe through the years. Carrie sleeping with her bare shoulder against a pure white sheet. Her hair was longer then, swept to one side to reveal the tiny tattoo at the base of her neck. The Swahili saying "hakuna wasiwasi" delicately scribed her attitude to life, "no worries".

We were travelling across Kenya at the time. The four of us sitting in a local tourist beauty parlour in Mombassa. Batik cushions covered wicker chairs that had seen better days.

A few large palms strategically placed to give privacy to the area where two young women were showing the designs to foreigners consumed with bravado and purposefulness to have their travels permanently etched on to their bodies. "Are you sure Cass?" I asked with genuine concern. "Yeh, sure, why not?"

She laughed throwing her head back, "Hattie and Jen are doing it as well". I knew there was no point trying to dissuade them. My three happy go-lucky friends taking a leap of faith that it would be alright, and it was. It was only me, and always me, that held back, overly cautious, afraid.

The date and location of the photo appears. Thursday December 31st, 2017, 2.25pm. The middle of the afternoon, it was indulgent, extravagant, unnecessary. The time of day when "normal" people were going about their business, shopping for a party, preparing for guests, getting a manicure ahead of a hard night partying. But Carrie is not normal. She is a chameleon, she changes colours, she changes allegiance, she adapts to changing circumstances.

Simmering anger makes its way through my body. A soaring heat consumes me, reaching my temple as beads of perspiration trickle across my brow. I turn off the phone and wipe it carefully with the hem of my t-shirt with trembling hands. Marcus must not know that I've discovered his sordid secret. I open his box hesitating, panic stricken. Had it been lying face down? At an angle? I can't be sure. He hadn't made any attempt to hide it, I consider. So, trusting, so under-estimating of me, that's Marcus. I close the lid and return it to its place. I have work to do.

Marcus

Life was sweet, considered Marcus, as he smoked a crafty cigarette at the far end of the garden away from Rachel's judging eyes. He sat in the wicker chair shaded by shrubs feeling smug. After months of cash flow challenges, he'd secured a buyer for the listed building he had refurbished. With the papers signed he could be back in the money in a couple of months.

He hadn't told Rachel yet, somehow it felt important to share this with Carrie first. She would see then that he wasn't a loser, a no-hoper. He was back to old Marcus, the person who seduced her, beguiled her, persuaded her, and changed her. Before they innocently shared his coat to ward off the cold, in this very garden, she'd had no secrets, no sides to her, no worries. He smiled at the thought of her tattoo and wanted to sweep her hair from her neck to kiss it.

He recalled her talking about how Rachel had wanted her to not get it done, overly protective, anxious. Typical Rachel he thought; straight, conventional, organised, boring. Carrie's disregard for rules and zest for life drew her to him like a magnet. They were the same, he reflected, or at least their shared secret had put them in the same mould. Truthfully, Marcus knew that it was *her* moral compass that had gone awry first, not his.

They were both drunk the night he enveloped her in his coat out of the cold and the rapid quick-fire sex that ensued could have been a moment never to be repeated or spoken about again. But it was Cass who had texted the flirtatious invite the following year, in an impromptu moment to test his response.

Unable to resist, he texted back playing her. Let's see if she'll go through with it. She's all talk and no action. "Ok you book the room and I'll see you there. I trust you're good with figures. have my accounts to do." Send.

Ten minutes passed before the familiar ping of a text coming through. "Hilton Park Lane. Don't bring your accountant. I don't do threesomes (smiley face).

Marcus inhaled, recalling the excitement of opening the hotel door to see her smiling as she put her index finger to her lips, before kissing him. "Shh... let's agree the rules first. No guilt. No contact in-between. No mention of friends. No falling for each other."

"Deal!" he said, kissing her before she'd finished speaking.

The phone rang in the distance. He heard Rachel's voice speaking to her mother and relaxed, knowing the call would be long and he would get at least another twenty minutes to himself.

"Hello darling, how are you?" Rachel's mother asked lightly. She knew of Rachel's troubles, hoping that things were sorting themselves out between her and Marcus. "And how are the twins?" she continued, trying not to show concern in her voice.

"Everything is fine Mum," Rachel reassured her. She continued, "In fact, I was wondering if you and Dad are around next weekend. I thought I might come and stay a few days with the babies." She too was masking the anxiety hidden inside. More lies. Marcus's lie had become her lie. She too had been drawn into a web of deceit with her parents, her friends, her husband, her colleagues at work. She hated him for bringing her down to his level. Everything was "fine" to all who asked. The glib vacuous saying was an easy cover-all response that demanded no further explanation. "How was your weekend?" Fine. "How are the boys?" Fine. "How are you?" Fine.

"Of course, you're welcome darling, anytime you know that. As it happens, Daddy and I are having a garden party, just the neighbours and a few friends from round and about. Bring Marcus if you want". She said, secretly hoping her errant son-in-law would not be available.

Rachel

The evening garden party was in full swing by the time Rachel had put the boys to sleep in the guest room of the two-hundred-year thatched cottage and her childhood home. She put the baby monitor on the wooden kitchen work top and stepped into the humid summer heat, looking around for her parents. She had deliberately not told Marcus about the party, knowing that a quiet weekend under her parents" scrutiny would be something he would avoid at all costs.

She felt freer than she had done for months and had taken extra care with her appearance. The short flowing pink silk dress clung in the right places and showed off the slim legs she had kept hidden during her pregnancy. Self-conscious, and aware that she knew few people, except for the couple who were her parent's oldest friends. She readily sipped the prosecco in her hand, admiring the rich hue of the myriad of flowers in the garden.

"It's a fantastic display, isn't it?" a male voice said from behind her. Rachel glanced round to catch the dazzling smile of John Howard. She remembered him from school. Tall, athletic, tanned, and somebody who had no clue as to who she was then or now. He extended his hand "Hi I'm John". She liked the firm grasp and managed to stop herself from letting him know that their paths had crossed, albeit during the giddy years of adolescence.

"Rachel". She returned the smile trying not to look at him directly. "So, what's your connection to the Greens? I must admit I'm a bit of a gate-crasher." He moved closer and whispered conspiratorially. "My parents live close-by, and I happened to be visiting. It was either Johnny no mates and a takeaway on my ownsome or joining them for a couple of hours. I must say, I haven't been here for years."

"You've been here before then?" Rachel asked intrigued. "Oh hardly. I delivered the papers here when I was at school". The image of a tall, dark haired boy with chiselled features, whistling as he cycled up the drive came to mind. She recalled how much she looked forward to Sunday mornings when she would take a glimpse through the curtains from her room, not daring to show her face.

"So, are you, local?" He enquired again. "Actually, I'm Charlotte and Andrew's daughter," she confessed, trying to curb the blush that was spreading across her face and neck. "Oh God, I'm so sorry," he said apologetically, adding "Would we have been at school together?" Yes of course we were she thought inwardly. I was the small, boring girl who was not part of the in-crowd. The one who no-one included in party invitations.

The one who was part of the wallpaper, silent, inconspicuous, silently observing but never participating. I sat two rows in front of you for registration, but the back of my head was as interesting as my face. Yes, we were at school together in the same class, but we may as well have been two hundred miles apart. This time, Rachel looked directly at him, noticing the green flecks in his eyes, and smiled "Yeh, we were at school together but that was a long time ago. Maybe we should just start over."

Rachel

"The sense of unhappiness is so much easier to convey than that of happiness. In misery we seem aware of our own existence, even though it may be in the form of a monstrous egotism: this pain of mine is individual, this nerve that winces belong to me and to no other. But happiness annihilates us: we lose our identity." ("The End of the Affair" – Graham Green)

I pile the baby clothes into the washer and bring down the suitcases from the loft. One for toys, one for me, one for them. Fear surrounds me. Fear that he'll find out. Fear of what he might do. Fear of the unknown. Fear for the future. I throw the blue bunny with the chewed off ear alongside a beanie dog in the case. No, they are favourites.

Too suspicious to disappear. I take them out and replace with less used toys. I'm panicking – stop it Rachel, I tell myself. I have got plenty of time, all day in fact. Marcus is at work, and I have the week off.

Executing my plan will take time and attention to detail is paramount. Luckily, it is one of my strengths, and a major weakness in Marcus. He delegates and expects everybody else to pay attention to the details. I deal with the paperwork at home, I make sure the bills are paid on time, I sort out the best deals for our mobiles and utilities.

I search through the kitchen drawer for a pair of scissors. They are part of my plan. Trepidation and intoxication sit side by side, the antithesis of six months of uncertainty, loneliness and hurt. It is late June, just six months after New Year's Eve in the hotel room where Marcus and I had spent the night together but what I now realise should have been for Carrie.

I make my way upstairs as each step feels heavy and my muscles ache. Packing is easy because I am so organised. It was one of those things that drives Marcus mad. My wardrobe is colour coordinated and sorted according to the seasons. Pastels and light weight jackets, trousers and dresses for Spring; linen and floaty dresses for Summer; heavier fabrics and darker separates for Winter.

I keep the clothes on their hangers and carefully cover them with zipped plastic covers. I keep some items in the wardrobe, just in case Marcus opens it. Shoes, so many shoes! Another source of irritation for Marcus. "Hakuna wasiwasi" I smile to myself remembering Carrie's tattoo. I put a selection of my favourites into the case and open a bin liner for the rest and leave an empty bin liner at the bottom of the wardrobe, this too is part of my plan.

It is raining outside. The first rain we have had for over six weeks and a perfect day to declutter. Marcus's wardrobe is neat and orderly too but only because I iron and hang up his shirts. Now that he has reverted to his old wardrobe and has left the grungy look behind, he is grateful that I do this for him, but he still takes it for granted.

How does he think his shirts miraculously make their way into his wardrobe, ironed, clean, ready for the week ahead, I wonder? I start at the back and pull out his casual shirts, then systematically work my way through every shirt hung carefully according to colour. It's surprising how long it takes to cut off every single button. Finally, I put them back as found and close the door behind me.

The gang are coming over later for our usual book group evening. I am looking forward to it even though I won't be there. I feel sorry for Jen and Hattie, but I hope they will find it entertaining before the betrayal sinks in. I am sitting at the kitchen table having a cup of tea and send out the usual reminder "Looking forward to the usual, later – 6.30pm. Drinks and taxi obligatory! Xx" Carrie gets the same message, but I think it's better for her to get here earlier, after all there's a lot to talk about. I give her a 6pm start which I know will not seem unusual as she knows I prefer an early night these days because of the babies. For extra pzazz, I have invited Ben, Rob, and Jack. All my friends together; it is important that they are all here to celebrate new beginnings, well three of them at least. I wish I could be a fly on the wall to observe, I consider smiling inwardly.

The fear is subsiding I note. Now that I am organised, I have regained control. The future is in my grasp, and I know now that change is empowering, static maintenance is disempowering. I have found myself finally; I am no longer the wall flower who was invisible to classmates; I know this because John Howard tells me he wants me. I want him but I am taking it slowly, my terms, my timeline, my control.

I put the cases in the boot and cover them with a rug. I am almost done.

Marcus

It is the book group get together this evening and Marcus is looking forward to seeing Carrie albeit fleetingly. He always goes to the pub after football, and it is an evening out of the house when he knows Rachel will be more preoccupied with her friends than watching the clock and having a go at him when he returns.

The long days are taking their toll, but the deal is almost closed now, and it's been worth putting in the extra hours to complete the refurbishment. He pulls into the drive and switches off the engine wondering what mood she will be in.

These days she could go from being on a complete high, to mono syllabic responses to his questions. He couldn't figure her out – surely, she'd be happy that he had got his act back together, their finances were improving, and he was happy to give her time to herself at the weekend, when he gladly took the boys out to the park.

The time that he got to see Carrie, if only at a distance but hopefully that would change this New Year's Eve when she realises these past few months were just a blip. Last New Year was also a blip he considered. He knew that guilt had begun to seep in, and Ben was beginning to be a bigger part in her life. Anyway, a lot can happen in six months and while Ben may not be around, he always would be.

Rachel opened the door as he put the key into the latch. "Hi darling," she said casually, allowing him to step inside. The kitchen looked immaculate. "Wow you've been busy." Marcus smiled kissing her on the lips lightly. He poured himself some tea from the pot looking around the gleaming surfaces. The babies were playing quietly with their books on a mat in the lounge. "If it's OK with you, I'll get a quick half hour in before I go to the pub. These early starts are catching up with me. I'll take a shower - could you wake me up in 30 minutes and I'll be out of your way."

Marcus was a creature of habit. He liked his regular cup of tea when he got in and then had a quick power nap before heading out on football nights. Rachel knew this, it was part of her plan. When Marcus fell asleep, nothing would wake him. Babies crying in the night, the wind howling, rain against the windowpane, her crying quietly into her pillow. "Sure OK, I'll wake you up just before six." He kissed her again and closed the door behind him.

She waited until she could hear the gentle snore from outside the door, indicating that Marcus had fallen into a deep and peaceful sleep. Quietly she opened the wardrobe door and took out the bin liner hidden at the back and filled it with one shoe from each pair that sat at the bottom of his wardrobe. For good measure, she picked up the remaining shoes and trainers under the bed and threw them in the plastic bag. The pettiness of the action would leave an immediate and satisfactory irritation but nothing in comparison to her long-term plan that would protect her future and the future of her babies.

She shut the door quietly and put the bag into the car and gathered her handbag, keys, mobile, and beanie dog and chewed rabbit, flinging them on to the front seat of the car. The boys were dressed and fed ahead of their journey back to Brighton, with any luck they would fall asleep, and she would be free to process her thoughts. What would they think? What would they say? Did they really think she was that stupid? She put the key into the ignition and quietly pulled out of the drive.

Finally, her secret will protect her. The secret of her babies' DNA. Her currency and her future. Her insurance policy where the stakes were high and investment costly. A secret that lay in the most unlikely person and an intangible interloper that would dictate her future.

Marcus was disorientated. He thought Rachel was ringing a bell outside, why would she do that? She only needed to open the curtains and wake him up with a cuppa. He roused, blinking and cocked his head to one side trying to process where the ringing was coming from. Irritated he got up and pulled on his jeans running down the stairs bare chested. The incessant doorbell forced him to prioritise opening the door, rather than check to see where Rachel was.

Carrie stood in the doorway with wet ringleted hair and soaked raincoat. "Oh, sorry Marcus, I didn't realise you were in. I was expecting Rachel. Sorry but it's pelting with rain and stupidly I forgot my umbrella" she said flushed at seeing him as she stepped inside. Still blurry from sleep he stepped aside "What the fu.." he said stopping in mid-sentence, noticing Jenna and Hattie walking up the garden path. Ben, Rob, and Jack greeted each other smiling, following in their footsteps with slight trepidation at the unusual gathering to which they had been summoned. The playful text from Rachel revealed nothing other than a small surprise party for Marcus. Now an ominous foreboding hovered above as they approached the doorway.

"Uhm, I'm not sure where Rachel is," Marcus said as the friends entered the kitchen looking around. "She may have gone for a walk with the babies." He offered the explanation knowing that it seemed unlikely. "But her car isn't here," Jenna announced, perturbed. It was then that a text came through to the mobile phones in their hands. "Sorry, change of plan. I'm sure you'll understand. This month's book to discuss is on the kitchen table" R.

A book lay open on the kitchen table *"A story has no beginning or end: arbitrarily one chooses that moment of experience from which to look back or from which to look ahead." Graham Green, The End of the Affair*

Table of Contents